THE MAPMAKER CHRONICLES

‹CHRONICLES›

BREATH OF THE DRAGON

D1017980

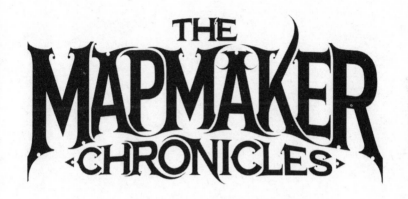

THE MAPMAKER CHRONICLES

BREATH OF THE DRAGON

A. L. TAIT

Kane Miller
A DIVISION OF EDC PUBLISHING

First American Edition 2017
Kane Miller, A Division of EDC Publishing

Copyright © A.L Tait, 2015

First published in Australia and New Zealand in 2015 by Hachette Australia
(an imprint of Hachette Australia Pty Limited), this North American edition
is published by arrangement with Hachette Australia Pty Ltd.

For information contact:
Kane Miller, A Division of EDC Publishing
P.O. Box 470663
Tulsa, OK 74147-0663
www.kanemiller.com
www.edcpub.com
www.usbornebooksandmore.com

Library of Congress Control Number: 2016955644

Printed and bound in the United States of America
7 8 9 10

ISBN: 978-1-61067-624-3

For Bev and Dennis

There for every step of the journey

Chapter One

"There's nothing here. Nothing green, no sign of animals, nothing. It's like this part of the world is dead."

Quinn Freeman shuddered at Ash's words. Dead. That's exactly what it looked like: bare rocks and shifting sands that stretched away towards a craggy, desolate mountain, the top of which was lost in dark, threatening clouds. Even the air smelled stale, with a tang of burning embers, coating his throat and making his eyes water all the time.

Ever since that first day when he'd been chosen for this crazy quest to map the world and prove it wasn't flat, he'd been waiting with dread to arrive at this place. For surely this was the end of the world? The only thing missing was Genesi, the fire-breathing dragon who awaited anyone silly enough to sail this far.

It wasn't that long ago that Quinn had decided that he had nothing to fear from Genesi. That the dragon was a mere story, and that people – such as the Gelynion explorer Juan Forden, who had kidnapped Quinn – were more to be feared. Now he was not so sure, and he was keeping a wary eye on that forbidding mountain, and the wreaths of dark smoke that encircled it.

The rocky shore looked yellow in the dying light of the sun; pale gold turning to burnished bronze, like the famed loganstones mined in a secret corner of Verdania. A breath of air ruffled Quinn's dark hair as he scanned the barren coastline, searching for something – anything – that could be eaten. All he could see were the strange piles of long white teeth dotted at intervals along the sand. Castoffs from Genesi?

A deep growl to his right startled him.

"What was that?" he asked, turning to face his friend Ash, who was now slumped morosely over the rail beside him.

"My stomach," she muttered, blushing.

Quinn managed a laugh. "And here I was thinking girls were such dainty creatures . . ."

Ash thrust her elbow at him roughly, catching him on the side of the jaw. "Ow," he said.

"Don't mess with me when I'm hungry, Quinn."

He rubbed his jaw ruefully, knowing that he'd deserved the jab. Weeks of surviving on little more than gruel-flavored water had left everyone on board the *Libertas* on edge. And Ash had even more reason to be anxious than the rest of the crew.

Quinn looked at her now, so skinny that her cheekbones seemed to slice across her skin – and yet he could still see the wiry strength in her. It was the same strength that had led her to stow away on the *Libertas* in the first place, that had seen her find a place as a healer amongst this group of hardened sailors, and had allowed her to stand up to those same sailors as she'd argued for her place aboard the ship.

"Still glad you came?" he asked her.

She looked at him sideways, eyes deep blue under her lashes.

"Yes," she said, simply. "Despite everything, even if this is the end of the world, it's better than being in the King's castle by myself."

He nodded. Ash's mother, Sarina, had died of a broken heart after being hounded from their home village for her knowledge of plants and healing, leaving Ash alone in Oakston, the biggest town in Verdania. It was only by chance that he and Ash had been reunited in the walled garden at the King's castle. Ash had found work at the castle, and Quinn had been chosen for scribe school, to learn to be a mapmaker under the instruction of Master Blau.

Quinn sighed now as he thought about how different his life would have been had Master Blau and Zain never knocked on the door of his family's whitewashed cottage in Markham. Instead of starving here, gazing hopelessly at a desolate shore, he'd be looking forward to a sizzling roast dinner with four kinds of vegetables and thick, steaming gravy.

Quinn loved his mam's gravy and had been helping her make it for years, which is how he knew that the secret ingredient was . . . He frowned. Was it a pinch of arrowroot? Or a teaspoon?

Wincing as a sharp pain shot through his head, he realized he couldn't remember. Which would not be a big deal if he wasn't Quinn. Because Quinn remembered *everything*, from every step of every one of his mam's recipes, to where he was on this day six years ago, to every detail of the maps he was creating on this journey. He held pictures in his mind of everything he ever saw or read or heard and when he wanted to remember, he simply flicked back through those pictures until he found the one he needed.

Although, since falling from a mast and banging his head while trying to escape from the Gelynions (and a boatload of pirates) a few weeks earlier, it was as though someone had torn strips from his picture book. The big pictures were still there, but some of the details were missing.

Ash had warned him that the knock to his head might have side effects, but he'd thought he'd just suffer a few flashes of pain for a day or two and it would all return to normal.

Days had stretched to weeks and the sharp pain came less frequently – but he was only just beginning to feel the full damage to his memory.

He hadn't told Ash about his worry. He'd decided to keep it to himself.

A deep rumble interrupted his thoughts, and Ash nudged him. "Who's dainty now?" she said with a laugh.

"That wasn't me!" he responded, more sharply than he intended as his eyes were once again drawn to the distant mountain. "Look!"

Ash clutched his arm as they both stared at the peak. The gloomy clouds around the barren peak were even thicker, swirling and billowing.

"Wh—what is it?" asked Ash, clutching Quinn's arm.

"I don't know," he shouted, as the deep rumble echoed once again. "But I don't think we should tarry here."

"Do you think it's Genesi?" whispered Ash. "Are we going to be eaten?"

"Well, you won't make much more than a mouthful," said a deep voice behind them. "Either of you."

Quinn turned to face his captain, his eyes traveling up to look into Zain's scarred, weathered face. The Deslonder was the tallest man Quinn knew – or one of them, he amended, thinking of Morpeth, the other Deslonder who, along with Juan Forden, had so recently been Quinn's captor aboard the Gelynion ship the *Black Hawk*.

"I'm becoming less of a mouthful by the day," Quinn retorted, pulling the loose waistband of his patched breeches up for emphasis.

"Have you spotted anything?" Zain asked, serious now. "Anything at all?"

"Nothing," said Ash, echoing her earlier words. "There's nothing edible anywhere. There's just rocks and sand and . . . that!" She gestured wildly in the direction of the mountain, still belching smoke but no longer creaking and groaning.

Zain frowned.

Quinn knew that his captain would be more worried about the crew's hunger than dragons, imagined or not. Zain was an intensely practical man who focused on the here and now, and one of the most difficult aspects of any expedition like this one was food supply. The possibility of starvation was always a passenger on a ship like the *Libertas*. That Zain, who had come to Verdania as a slave more than twenty years before, had pleaded with his King for the opportunity to take part in this race to map the world, handpicking his crew for the journey, only made it worse. He'd brought them all to this place.

His prize of choice was freedom, not just for him but for every man aboard the *Libertas*. Quinn, whose father was a freehold farmer, had not fully appreciated the magnitude of this prize until his own freedom had been taken from him by Forden and Morpeth. But he was also beginning to understand the price they might all pay for the opportunity to compete for the prize.

Quinn wondered if the other two explorers – Dolan, the former mercenary who had chosen gold as his prize, and Odilon, who was competing for a seat on the King's Council and the power that went with it – were experiencing the same hardships. He hoped that Ajax, Odilon's cheerful redheaded mapmaker, was okay. The last time he'd seen his friend, Odilon had been leading Ajax away into the dark, having handed Quinn over to the Gelynions and stolen a copy of his map.

When it came to the third mapmaker, however, Quinn couldn't help but hope that noble, blond Ira was at least hungry. If not starving. And wet. And cold. And locked in a dark room pleading for mercy. And . . .

"Have you checked the calculations today?"

Zain's voice broke into Quinn's thoughts, and the pleasurable image of Ira broken and alone faded. Quinn would not soon forgive the other boy for pushing him down into a pit so that Quinn could be taken captive by Juan Forden. Actually, make that *never* forgive.

"I have," Quinn answered Zain now. He had spent the afternoon checking wind speed, the angle of the sun, and the estimated drag of the ocean. "It's all there." Quinn had taken greater care than usual when adding the details to the captain's manifest, knowing he couldn't rely on his memory.

Some days he wanted to scream in frustration about the tattered edges of his once-perfect memory, but to do so would bring attention to it. Better, he thought, to wait. Surely he would recover soon?

Zain exhaled loudly, his own frustration apparent, though it was focused on the lack of stores aboard the *Libertas*. "The sun will soon be gone," he said. "Let us turn in for tonight and hope that the morning light brings better views." He did not mention an evening meal and Quinn and Ash knew better than to ask.

"I'll just check on Cleric Greenfield before I go to bed," said Ash. "He is becoming more frail each day and it worries me."

The elderly cleric had been sent with them by the King to "supervise" Zain, and was a kind and gentle presence on the *Libertas*. Quite what the King had thought he might do to stop Zain from setting sail for the sunset and never returning to Verdania, nobody knew, but, as no one on board would ever do anything to upset the cleric or disrupt their quest, it was a moot point.

"And I," said Zain, shaking his head. "I have tried to make him take extra portions, but he will not."

Ash smiled as she took her leave. "No, he wouldn't."

Quinn knew she was very fond of the grizzled little man, who had provided much solace for her when Quinn had been kidnapped.

"He never, ever doubted that you would come back," she'd told Quinn in such a wide-eyed way that Quinn suspected Ash may have had a moment or two of uncertainty. Quinn couldn't blame her for that. He'd had several long, dark moments of doubt of his own and the blackness that he'd felt inside himself during those times had frightened him more than Genesi ever could.

Then again, Quinn thought, looking once again at the rocks, that was before he'd found himself here, where the dying orange light was as fiery as a dragon's flames, and the earth looked scorched and desolate, as though laid waste by a dragon's smoky breath.

He had thought their quest would end in a rush of water as they fell off the edge of the world, but maybe this wasteland, where nothing could grow or survive, was it and they would simply fade away.

Quinn rubbed his eyes. His head was beginning to hurt again and the lack of food was making him so very, very tired.

"Are you all right, Quinn Freeman?" Zain asked.

"Just hungry."

Zain eyed him closely. "You have not been yourself."

"No," he said, managing a smile. "I'm about half of myself right now, I think."

Zain did not laugh. "You have been through a lot," he said. "We have asked a lot of you. I knew that you did not want to do this and –"

"You said you needed me," said Quinn, quietly. "You still do."

Zain's faith in him, in his memory, as an important tool in winning his freedom, was one reason that Quinn didn't feel he could tell him about the problems he was having.

"I do," said Zain. "We all do –"

"Then there's nothing more to say," Quinn interrupted, glad that the lengthening shadows meant that Zain could not clearly see his face, which was screwed up against the tears pricking the backs of his eyes and the throbbing pain beginning in his head. "I will do my best, Zain. I promised you. I promised my da."

Zain nodded, reaching over and grasping Quinn by the shoulder. "I know you will," he said. "For now, though, to bed."

Quinn nodded. "I'm going to dream of bacon," he said, forcing joviality into his voice. "And, er . . ." He paused a moment, flailing about mentally to remember the word he wanted, while Zain looked at him closely. "Griddle cakes," Quinn said triumphantly as it popped into his head.

"Hmm," his captain said. "Well, make sure your dreams don't keep you up all night salivating – you seem tired."

"With any luck they'll make me feel so full I'll sleep until the breakfast bell," said Quinn, scuttling away before the conversation could go any deeper.

Tiredness was the least of his problems.

Chapter Two

Quinn awoke with a start as dawn crept in through the porthole. On the other side of the cabin, Tomas muttered in his sleep, his hammock swinging slightly as he shifted position.

Quinn could remember a time when he'd enjoyed the solitude of his little cabin, but it had been many moons since it had been his alone. First Kurt had moved in when the Verdanians had rescued him from certain death in an icy village in the frozen north – that had not been the most comfortable time of Quinn's voyage.

Then, after Quinn's return to the *Libertas*, Zain had decided, much to Quinn's relief, that the two boys needed to be separated and had sent Kurt down to the hold with the other crew members. Tomas had joined them in Barbarin, his passage to Verdania paid for with jewels his own father had stolen from King Orel, and he was proving to be a much easier cabinmate.

Quinn stared up at the wooden planks above his bed, every muscle on high alert. What had woken him?

The thumping of running boots answered the question. Quinn froze. The last time he'd heard sounds like that, he'd been locked in the dark hold of the *Black Hawk* as pirates invaded. Surely it could not be happening again?

He sat up, feeling around in the half-light for his boots. Tomas murmured but did not wake, and Quinn wondered at his friend's ability to sleep through such a racket. Then again, Tomas had been a pirate in training himself, so maybe he'd grown used to such noise.

"*Leif's boots*," Quinn cursed under his breath, unable to locate his left boot. Zain was always going on at them about wearing their boots, saying that a sailor without them was always on the back foot. There was even a rumor that their captain slept in his own worn brown footwear – but Quinn couldn't bring himself to do that.

He finally found the offending boot at the other end of the bed, where it must have slid with the rolling motion of the ship, and pulled it on. Overhead, all was quiet. Quinn breathed a sigh of relief. Had it been pirates that had caused the earlier crash, he'd be hearing sounds of a fight by now.

Unless they'd killed everybody on deck?

By the time he'd taken a sharp intake of breath at the thought, Quinn had jumped to his feet and was out the door and racing headlong down the passageway.

Up the stairs he hurtled, bursting out into the cool morning air – and straight into Cleaver, Zain's first mate.

"Whoa," said Cleaver, readjusting his customary bandanna. "Where's the fire?"

Quinn looked around wildly. "I thought – I just – What was that crash I heard?" he finished lamely, realizing that there was nobody on deck but himself and the crusty old salt.

Cleaver rolled his eyes. "Kurt," he said, succinctly. Quinn knew that the older man wasn't fond of the Northern boy either, though Cleaver's dislike stemmed more from Kurt's laziness and surly attitude than from suspicion or distrust. An honest, hardworking man himself, Cleaver had no time for anyone who wouldn't "muck in" as he called it, and Kurt had shown no interest in taking part in the hard graft of keeping the *Libertas* afloat. These days, Kurt had been given regular jobs to complete, but his first weeks on board, when he'd moped around doing nothing, stuck in Cleaver's mind like a thorn.

"What did he do this time?" Quinn asked.

"Only dropped the birdcage so that it broke and all the birds flew out," said Cleaver with a sigh. "Abel and I had a swine of a time trying to catch them."

He pointed to the hastily repaired cage on the deck alongside the main mast. The bird population had been reduced to three. It must have been the crash of the cage hitting the deck that had woken Quinn, and the thumping he'd heard was Cleaver and Abel trying to catch the birds.

Quinn breathed a sigh of relief. The loss of the birds wasn't ideal, but there was no threat to the *Libertas*. "At least we don't need them at the moment," he said to Cleaver. "We're in sight of land anyway."

The birds were an ingenious navigation method that Quinn had picked up on board the *Black Hawk*. They were released to help ships find land, the premise being that the birds would always fly towards solid ground.

"That's true enough for now," agreed Cleaver. "But for how long? When I think of all the trouble that Dilly and Ison had capturing more birds in the first place, I could wring that blasted boy's neck."

Before Quinn could offer his assistance, Kurt appeared, blue eyes narrowed in his small, pale face.

"Tell him it was an accident," he said to Quinn in Suspite, nodding towards Cleaver. The Northern boy spoke no Verdanian and could communicate only with Quinn and Zain, who both spoke Suspite, the language at the heart of all others.

Quinn stared at him before relaying the information to Cleaver, who harrumphed.

"Tell *him*," said Cleaver, "that there are all together too many accidents when he's around and that he ought to think more about what he's doing."

Quinn took great pleasure in relaying Cleaver's words, but Kurt merely smirked and sloped off towards the bow, confirming Quinn's suspicions that he did these things on purpose. Whether he was just trying to get out of doing jobs he disliked or whether there was a more sinister motive, Quinn wasn't sure. But to be safe, he was actually creating two maps – a real one that was as true and detailed as he could make it, and a fake one, that would ensure that anyone who used it would run aground or end up lost. The real one was hidden down in Cleric Greenfield's cabin, and the gentle old man was the only other person in the world who knew of its existence.

His mistrust of Kurt had been reinforced when Quinn had overheard Odilon and Juan Forden talking about how they'd gotten their hands on Quinn's map – Kurt had copied it and given it to them. Unfortunately, there were no other witnesses to that conversation, the map had ostensibly remained on board the *Libertas* the whole time Quinn had been on the *Black Hawk*, and Quinn had been unable to convince Zain of Kurt's guilt.

"You have no proof," Zain had said. He'd also tried to explain to him that Kurt couldn't help his animosity, that the anger and grief at losing everything he'd ever known had consumed Kurt, making him lash out at those nearest – in this case, his rescuers – but Quinn thought that Zain was altogether too understanding at times.

"I know how he feels," Zain had said, simply. "I have been there."

And that was that. The story of Zain's arrival in Verdania was shrouded in mystery – mostly because Zain never spoke of it, and nobody else seemed to know anything. Quinn knew that he'd once been a proud warrior until he was captured in the Crusadic Wars some twenty years before and had appeared in King Orel's palace. He also knew, because he'd seen it for himself, that Zain's relationship with the King looked more like friendship than a master/slave dynamic.

Quinn was startled back to the present by a shout from above. Peering up, shading his eyes against the growing strength of the sun, Quinn could make out Abel's big feet hanging over the side of the watch platform. "People!" the sailor shouted. "People ahead!"

People? Quinn's gaze shifted to the shore, which looked no less desolate than it had the night before. There was no sign of life. What had Abel seen? And just how far "ahead" was it?

"Cleaver!" came Zain's bellow from the wheelhouse. "Take the wheel!"

Cleaver hurried to do his captain's bidding and Zain was at the bottom of the main mast in moments. Quinn joined him.

"Abel!" Zain shouted. "Get down here."

Within a heartbeat, Quinn could hear the familiar slide-thump noise that accompanied a man's travels up and down the mast. Abel hit the deck.

"I can't see any sign of people," said Zain, waving his arm in the direction of the coast.

"Leagues away," puffed Abel. "Ahead. It must be people. Or very large ants."

Zain grimaced. "Ants?"

"They're moving like ants," said Abel. "Scores of them."

Zain shook his head, turning to Quinn. "Go up and see what you can see," he said. "Abel may be suffering hunger hallucinations."

Quinn hid a grin at Abel's outraged expression, and grabbed hold of the mast.

"Take it easy," Zain added. "Lack of food weakens a man – and you are not yet a man."

Now it was Abel's turn to smirk as Quinn bit back several retorts. Moments later, as he began his climb, he had to concede that Zain was right. Every day without solid food sapped his strength a little more. If it went on too much longer, he'd struggle to get up the mast at all.

Clambering onto the watch platform, Quinn held tight to the mast with his left hand, using his right to shade his eyes as he looked about him. To his left, the sea sparkled in the sunshine, clear and smooth as far as the eye could see. To his right, he could see nothing but rocks, sand

and, far from the shore, a line of stubby, stunted bushes, stretching out to the base of that monstrous peak. It was a cruel, dry landscape offering no hope.

Quinn peered ahead, where the shoreline seemed to rise into a series of low cliffs, and frowned. Here, the land narrowed, and he could see a shadow not far from the top, as though the earth gave way to darkness. As he watched, Quinn became aware of something moving in the landscape.

He blinked. It was hard to make out what they were, as they were the same color as the sand, but judging by the size, he could only assume Abel was right. He was looking at people.

Or very large ants.

"Well?" came Zain's impatient voice from below.

Quinn hung his head over the edge of the platform so that he could better talk to Zain. "Definitely people. Well, almost definitely." Abel's triumphant "Ha!" wafted up to his ears.

There was a long pause. "A village?" asked Zain.

"No sign of any kind of buildings," said Quinn. "Just people."

"How far?"

"Half a day's sail," Quinn guessed. "Maybe less."

"Less!" shouted Abel. "People mean food. With food on offer, we can get there quicker."

Zain laughed. "Their food will not make our ship sail faster, but we will try. Trim the sails!"

As Quinn watched, the deck below swarmed with activity as the crew rushed up from below decks to follow their captain's orders. As he began the climb down the mast, stomach growling in protest at the use of energy, he prayed that Abel was right – he'd like breakfast sooner rather than later.

He could only hope that the locals were friendly.

Chapter Three

"I don't think they like us."

Tomas muttered the words so that only Quinn and Ash could hear.

"What makes you say that?" Quinn whispered back sarcastically, staring at the wall of silent, watchful men. Dressed alike in the same dun-colored tunics, covered in dust and holding large shovels, the men looked like something out of the fairy tales his mam used to tell him – sand goblins, perhaps.

Quinn and Tomas were standing behind Zain on a narrow beach at the foot of the cliffs that Quinn had spotted from the mast. Abel stood, tense and ready, by the longboat just a few paces down the beach.

Looking up at the sandy-colored cliffs, Quinn could see that they were irregularly marked with deep shadows, indicating caves. Given that he had spotted no sign of a village nearby, he couldn't help but wonder if the caves were home to these men – and there had to be at least fourscore of them.

Dotted along the base of the cliffs were the remains of five large fires, marked out by those strange long teeth that Quinn had noticed piled up along the coast. He was itching to go over for a closer look at them, but suspected that he'd probably get a shovel across the head if he so much as coughed right now.

Behind them, in the shallow waters, the *Libertas* bobbed merrily in the dazzling sunshine. Here in the shadows of the cliffs, the mood was much cooler, and the air smelled staler than ever.

"Who is your leader?" Zain asked again, his voice as patient as if he were dealing with a difficult toddler.

Still the men said nothing, staring at the *Libertas* group as though they were ghosts. Zain had brought only Quinn, Tomas and Abel with him, despite arguments from the rest of the crew. And Ash.

"You must stay here with the cleric," Zain had told her firmly. "He is ill and he needs you." She had nodded, but Quinn had taken one look at her mulish face and known that he would be hearing about the injustice of this for a long time to come.

"As for the rest of you, if I have learned one thing from this journey it is not to take all my best men in the first advance," Zain continued.

Quinn thought back to their previous experiences – Ash having to rescue them all from a tribal village, Dolan and Ira stealing all their food, Odilon stealing his map, just for starters – and couldn't help but agree with this tactic.

Personally, he'd have been happy to stay on board. His head was hurting, hunger was making him irritable and, frankly, he couldn't understand why Zain continued to ignore the fact that he needed to protect his mapmaker. "Without the mapmaker you have no map," he constantly reminded his captain.

But Zain always came up with a good reason why he needed Quinn at hand. "Quinn, you're with me," he'd said that morning, holding up his hand to forestall the boy's protest. "I may need your languages."

And Quinn had sighed. He couldn't argue with that. It was Quinn's knack for languages that had gotten them out of trouble on more than one occasion. He was now fluent in Verdanian, Suspite, Deslondic (not that anyone but Zain had cottoned on to that), Gelynion, and a strange tribal language he'd learned overnight on one memorable occasion. He also knew a smattering of Renz, and, unbeknownst to Kurt, even a few words of the strange, garbled Northern language – mostly curse words, which he couldn't wait to share with Ajax (who had been at him to come up with an alternative to *Leif's boots* for some time). Tomas had begun teaching him Barbarese, along with the fascinating muddle of tongues that comprised what he called Prate – the language of pirates.

"Tomas, you come as well, Barbarese might be needed here," Zain said, "and I'm not sure Quinn's up to speed on that yet."

Quinn had looked down at his feet. It was true that Barbarese and Prate were taking him much longer to master than they should – mostly due to his fraying memory. But he was making light of it by pretending that he wasn't working hard at learning them. With any luck, the effects of the blow to his head would wear off soon and it would all just fall into place.

Now he sighed, realizing that the silent men were not responding to Suspite, Verdanian or Deslondic at all. Even as he had the thought, Zain motioned him forward.

"We are here in peace," Quinn said, in a loud, clear voice – first in Gelynion, then Renz. Nothing. He tried a few Northern words, although they also elicited no response – even the ones that he suspected were very derogatory. In desperation, he spoke in the clicks and whistles he'd learned to speak in the tribal village. Nothing.

"Tomas!" Zain beckoned.

Tomas stepped forward. "Good morning," he said in his native tongue. "We are hungry." He raised an imaginary bowl before him and tucked into it with an invisible spoon, pretending to eat something delicious.

The men stared through him.

"Try the Prate," said Quinn, in desperation.

Tomas looked at him strangely. "They don't look like pirates."

"Just try," he said. "And tell them you want to buy something."

Zain nodded. "Good thinking, Quinn."

So Tomas told the men, in Prate, that the Verdanians were in the market for food.

Eyebrows raised, the men looked at each other.

"They understand you," Quinn said in Verdanian. "Keep going."

"And say what?" Tomas asked, arms folded.

"Enough to prove to them that we are pirates, of course," said Quinn. "They've dealt with pirates before. We don't just want food – we want to trade treasure for . . . what do pirates trade for?"

"Usually they'll trade what they've stolen for food and weapons," said Tomas, conversationally.

"That then," said Quinn, cutting him off.

Tomas began spinning a story in Prate about how they had some merchandise they needed to off-load and how they'd be willing to trade for food and weapons. But just as the sand goblins, as Quinn had come to think of them, began to look interested, the earth beneath Quinn's feet began to move and that deep, echoing rumble he'd heard the night before shook the grains of sand.

The sand goblins looked at each other in consternation.

Before Quinn could instruct Tomas to ask what was going on, there was a commotion at the back of the group, which parted down the middle, allowing a small, sweating man to push his way through. Unlike the rest of the group, he was clean and groomed, his wiry gray hair sticking out around his head like a halo, reminding Quinn of his mother's silkie chickens. At first glance, he was richly dressed, wearing a dark-red jacket and dark-gray pants. As he came closer, however, Quinn could see there was a fine sheen of dust over his clothes, which did not fit him and were fraying at the collar and cuffs.

"You are?" the man queried in Prate, without niceties. He directed the question at Zain, looking over the heads of Quinn and Tomas to where he presumed the power lay.

"This is . . . Hayreddin," Tomas cut in quickly, not wanting the man to know that Zain could not speak Prate.

Quinn, who was only just keeping up himself, raised his eyebrows as Tomas nudged him to play along. He nodded, noting that the rumbling had subsided and the sand goblins had relaxed – a little.

"Hayreddin?" said the man.

"Hayreddin," Tomas said, firmly, "who used to be a lieutenant with the Golden Serpent." He then performed a complicated hand signal, while Quinn watched on, amazed. He wished he'd known that hand signal during his time on the *Black Hawk*, when the pirate known as the Golden Serpent had invaded the ship.

The man inhaled sharply, and then bowed. "It is an honor. I am Egunon, overseer of this operation on behalf of the chieftains."

Chieftains?

"Do you speak Suspite?" Quinn asked in that language. He was only picking up one word in two in Prate, and he needed a better idea of what was happening.

Egunon turned and appraised him with cool brown eyes. "I do," he said, and Quinn breathed a sigh of relief, even as he filed away the thought that the man had not responded to that language earlier. At least he and Zain would both know exactly what was going on.

"We prefer to conduct our trades in Suspite," said Zain, stepping forward. "Less room for error that way, don't you think?"

Egunon stared up as the huge Deslonder loomed over him, and nodded mutely.

"Very well then," said Zain. "Perhaps you would like to send your men back to their business, and we can parley."

Egunon hesitated briefly before turning to bark a short series of orders at the sand goblins.

Quinn exhaled. Forget errors, there was much less room for sudden attacks if the men were sent back to their work at the tops of the cliffs. The Verdanians had watched from the water as they'd swarmed down at first sight of the *Libertas*, and Quinn had once again been reminded of Abel's "large ants" description.

"What is it that you do here?" Zain asked, politely.

Egunon eyed him up and down, before allowing his eyes to drift to the *Libertas* anchored a short distance away.

"Come," he said, turning to follow his men up the cliffs. "I'll show you."

It seemed that Egunon had the same concerns about a sudden attack from the *Libertas* as they'd had about his men. Quinn met Zain's eyes, and his captain nodded that they should follow the smaller man.

"It may be a trap," said Tomas, quietly. "I have seen this before. We will be separated from our backup if we go up there."

"Are you coming?" Egunon said, impatiently. "Whatever you want is up there. Food, stones, supplies. Not here."

Zain frowned, whispering to Quinn: "Did you not say that there was no village?"

"None," Quinn confirmed.

"Then where are they keeping the supplies?"

"I have no idea," said Quinn. "I'm more interested in what he meant when he said stones."

"Are you kidding?" joked Tomas. "I stopped at food."

Quinn elbowed him, suppressing his laughter. "This is serious," he said.

"Yes," said Zain. "It is. Pull yourselves together and let's go and see what we've stumbled across here."

"Are we all going?" asked Quinn, watching the men

who were struggling up the rocky path that snaked its way along the cliff face.

"No," said Zain, decisively. "Tomas, go back to the *Libertas* with Abel. Tell them what's happening and then report back to the beach – bring Dilly, Jericho and Ison with you."

Quinn felt better at the thought that the battle-hardened crew members would soon be at their backs. Dilly, fast and nimble; Jericho, good-natured, but handy with his fists; Ison, who never backed down from a fight.

The only downside to all this was that Quinn was going to climb the cliffs with Zain. But he knew better than to voice his doubts.

He frowned now, thinking back to Decision Day. The day when three very different explorers had chosen their mapmakers for this journey. Whereas a few weeks ago, he'd have been able to describe every word, every detail, every note that the trumpet player had blown, now he just had a general overview of the day, a feeling. But even his dodgy memory was able to summon up Zain's words: "If I could do it without you, I would. But you have something I need."

The irony was, Quinn thought as he trudged over the sand at Zain's heels, he no longer had that special thing – his memory. Meaning he was out here, in danger, for nothing.

Chapter Four

Breathing hard, Quinn finally made it to the top of the cliff, feeling the climb in every one of his tired, under-nourished muscles. The sun beat down on top of his head, toasting his ears, and sweat dripped off his nose. He'd had to concentrate hard during the ascent, putting one foot in front of the other, one hand after another on the burning sand. Still, he'd been unable to resist trying to peer into one or two of those dark shadows he'd spotted from the beach, confirming that they were, indeed, caves – and deep ones, he decided, because he could see nothing but black beyond the openings.

He hauled himself over the lip of the cliff and lay gasping like a landed fish, wondering why the sand goblins hadn't made the path easier to traverse. In sections, it was quite easy walking, but progress between each level could be managed only by climbing through a series of shallow foot- and handholds – a journey made even more precarious with the cliff face shuddering under the assault of another of those scary rumbling noises. It had happened only once during the climb, but that had been enough to focus Quinn's efforts on climbing faster.

Now, he took in the view before him, and gasped. The sand goblins had swarmed back to their work in a landscape that seemed even more brutal and desolate than what they'd passed in the *Libertas* so far. Churned up and cut out, the ground disappeared about fifty paces in, disintegrating into a wide hole about shoulder deep on the men. Some of them were in the hole, passing up buckets of dirt, while others were pouring it into the shallow wooden dishes he'd spotted before. Now, however, Quinn noticed there were fine holes in the bottoms of the dishes, and that dirt was falling through the holes as the men swirled the dishes around, peering intently inside them. Over to the right, men with shovels were working hard, sending showers of dirt into the air, digging a new hole.

Quinn's eyes widened further as a huge beast reared up out of the hole, dragging a massive rock behind it on a rope. It was hard to tell what color it was under the dirt, but its ears were as wide as his mam's favorite bedsheets and it seemed to have a hose attached to the front of its face. On either side of that hose were two huge white teeth, just like those piled all along the coast.

He nudged Zain, who was also standing openmouthed, staring at the animal. A sand goblin was sitting cross-legged on the creature's back, using a short stick to slap it around the flanks, urging it forward. The beast strained up the side of the pit, its feet sliding from under it in the mud, making a wild, trumpeting sound that nearly deafened Quinn.

Quinn wished Ajax was there to capture the moment in a sketch, particularly as he was afraid his damaged memory wouldn't hold on to it long enough to describe it to his friend later.

Nobody else paid the racket any mind at all, continuing their digging and sifting as though they saw sights like this every day. Quinn blinked as the animal finally gained purchase on the sludgy ground and made it clear of the pit, mud drying on its wrinkled skin even as it stepped away from the hole and began trudging its way across the barren land, towards the faraway mountain.

While Quinn watched, the clouds around the top of the peak swirled and danced – parting enough for him to see that the top of the mountain was dripping rivers of fire.

He swallowed back a shout, instead freezing and pointing mutely, unable to form the words to tell Zain that the mountain was melting – or, perhaps, Genesi was rising from her lair.

Zain touched his shoulder. "I see it, Quinn Freeman," he said, "but look around you."

The sand goblins were paying the mountain no heed, and Quinn began to wonder if the fire-breathing mountain was simply an everyday occurrence.

He heard a shout and dragged his eyes from the sight, to see one of the dusty men running over to a large board lying on the left-hand side, holding his sifting dish high.

Quinn wrinkled his nose as he realized that the table was spread with what looked like a thick layer of pig fat.

Once there, the man shook the contents of his dish over the table, as three other men crowded around. Three of them lifted the board vertically and the fourth poured water down its face, as they all watched anxiously.

As the water flowed, Quinn could see that there were three rocks, each about the size of a quail's egg, still stuck to the table. To his surprise, all four men cheered and started hugging each other.

"Why are they so happy?" he asked Egunon, who was standing beside Quinn and Zain, watching the proceedings.

"They are one step closer to home," was all the small man said.

Zain frowned. "I see no food here," he said. "Only rocks. And . . . that." He pointed at the large beast, which was still lumbering off across the barren dirt, the boulder bouncing along behind it.

Quinn desperately wanted to ask what it was called, just as he wanted to know more about the mountain, but the time was not right. He had to wait for the official parley to begin to ask questions.

Egunon smiled, a thin, mean little smile. "You see only what I want you to see," he said. "Tell me more about this trade and then we will talk more about what you can see."

Quinn grimaced. What would Zain do now? The truth was that there was little to trade on the *Libertas*. Unlike Odilon, who had outfitted the *Fair Maiden* with silks and velvets, wine and silverware – even solid gold door handles until they'd been "liberated" at the tribal village – Zain had taken a utilitarian approach to stocking his ship. Quinn was pretty sure that Egunon wouldn't be very interested in their wooden bowls, cotton sheets and a hold that contained the last vestiges of their oats.

To Quinn's surprise, Zain's hand shot out and wrapped itself around Egunon's neck. His captain seemed to grow taller, wider and infinitely more menacing. He was, Quinn realized with a start, turning himself into "Hayreddin."

"My men and I are hungry," Zain growled, his deep, rumbling voice taking on a tone that Quinn had never heard before. "We have been at sea for many months and our holds are as full of treasure as our bellies are empty. Now, shall we discuss food – or shall I show you a little trick I learned from the Golden Serpent?"

Judging by the sudden whiteness of Egunon's face, he'd been privy to one or two of the Golden Serpent's little tricks before. He opened his mouth to scream to his men.

Zain's fingers tightened around his neck – not, Quinn noticed, enough to really hurt the man, but more than enough to make breathing a chore and to give Egunon a taste of Zain's strength. He seemed to change his mind about screaming.

"Ha!" Egunon squeaked. "Of course, of course."

His face reddened with the effort of speaking, and Zain loosened his grip, without letting go completely.

"If you'll just remove your hand, we can talk terms," Egunon said.

Zain relented, with a smile that made Egunon shiver. Quinn suppressed his own grin – Zain really did need to work on his friendly face.

Egunon looked at him, suspiciously. "You said you wanted to trade."

"And we do," said Zain. "You show us what you have for us, then we'll talk terms."

"Even the Golden Serpent does not work that way," said Egunon, edging backward. "He brings gold. Are you sure you worked with him?"

Zain looked at Quinn, a faintly alarmed expression in his eyes. "Of course," he said. "You want me to prove it?" He reached for the smaller man's neck again.

"Yes," said Egunon, in panic. "But not like that. Tell me something about him that only one of his crewmen would know."

Zain paused. "He painted his teeth gold."

Egunon rolled his eyes. "Everyone knows that. Something else."

Zain paused again, before regathering, standing over Egunon with a threatening look on his face. "Bah!" he shouted. "I'll show you his favorite method of torture if you like."

Quinn looked around nervously, noting that the men were starting to take notice of the confrontation. "His eyes are two different colors," he blurted out, surprising himself. "One almost black, one amber. He wears a patch on the black one."

The memory of the Golden Serpent climbing up the mast after him, trying to prevent his escape from the *Black Hawk*, had hit him in a flash. Gone were the days when Quinn could methodically go back through pictures in his mind to find the one he wanted – now he had to hope they crashed into place when he needed them.

Quinn only hoped that his memory had gotten this right – and that would be enough detail for Egunon as he couldn't recall anything more about the famed pirate.

Egunon hissed with recognition, and his whole manner transformed in an instant as Quinn exhaled in relief.

"Any friend of the Golden Serpent is of course a friend of mine," Egunon said. Bowing, he gestured for Zain and Quinn to follow, shouting something at the group of men still celebrating near the table. Around them, Quinn was relieved to note, the other men went back to their digging.

"Nice work," Zain muttered as they followed Egunon back down the path, passing a large, square hole that was fortified with petrified white wood.

"You're welcome," Quinn whispered out of the side of his mouth. "Hayreddin."

"I make an excellent pirate," said Zain, sounding slightly injured.

"A little too convincing," Quinn said with a small smile. "I don't remember seeing that throat grab in training."

Zain's "harumph" lifted the hair on the back of Quinn's neck as they descended. "A man cannot fight if he cannot breathe, Quinn Freeman. You would do well to remember that."

Egunon walked along the cliff face, disappearing into one of the dark openings.

"Stand aside," Zain said, as they reached the mouth of the cave. "I'll go first."

Thinking that was the best idea he'd heard all day, Quinn stood to one side as Zain ducked into the dark. Looking down at the beach, Quinn could see the *Libertas* crew, standing alert beside the longboat. He picked out Tomas in his bright-red shirt, one of a collection his mother had made for him, and Jericho standing beside him, his moustache creating a shadow on his face. Quinn frowned as he realized there were five small figures on the beach – not the expected four. Ash had not followed Zain's instructions to the letter,

Quinn thought with an inward smile . . . though he did wonder that she'd left the cleric's side. Still, reassured by their presence, he took one last look at the sun, and stepped into the darkness.

Chapter Five

It was cool, dark and quiet inside, and Quinn could detect the faintest scent of sizzling meat. Mouth watering, he felt his way along the walls, noting how the sand beneath his feet muffled the sound of his boots. While Zain had needed to bend almost double to get inside, Quinn had only to bow his head for the first few paces, before the tunnel opened up and he could stand. Reaching above his head, he couldn't touch the roof.

Taking a deep breath, he forced himself to walk forward. Zain had disappeared from sight, swallowed up by the blackness. Quinn shuddered. He hated the dark, and he fancied he could hear creaking and groaning in the tunnel walls.

"Zain," he whispered in Verdanian.

"Why are you whispering?" his captain boomed back, sounding no more than ten paces ahead of him.

"I'm just –"

"I'm pretty sure they know we're here, Quinn Freeman," came Zain's response, and Quinn could hear the quiver of laughter in his deep voice.

"It's very dark."

"Yes, it is," said Zain. "Keep walking. Follow my voice."

Quinn had no choice but to do so. As much as he was tempted to retreat back to the light, bright cave opening, his captain needed him.

"Keep coming," Zain said. "There are just two or three bends and then I think you'll like what you see."

Reassured, Quinn picked up his pace, continuing to run one hand along the wall. One bend, two bends, a longer stretch, a curve and then . . .

"*Leif's boots!*" he said, stepping into the light – and into a cavernous space. A hole in the roof allowed sunlight to stream in, bouncing and sparkling on the crystals in the walls. It was as though the stars had been brought underground.

"Indeed," said Zain.

Staring up, Quinn realized that the opening above their heads was the same fortified square they'd passed on the way to the cliff path. These people must have tunneled their way down through the rock to create the light well – he had a sudden sobering thought about what it must have been like to be the worker who had broken through that final layer of rock and fallen thirty or forty paces to the hard stone floor below.

Around them now, women and children went about their business, all dressed in the same dun-colored shifts as the men overhead. In one corner, a huge fire roared inside a carved stone hearth, adding to the stifling heat. It reminded Quinn of the cozy corner fireplace at the Fox & Glove in Markham, but here, there were no men warming their hands with mulled wine – instead, a large joint of meat was being roasted, turned regularly on a pole by two young boys with hot, sooty faces.

At the end of the chamber, a row of seven arches led into darkness. Perhaps that was where the food was stored? Or the sleeping quarters? Or both? Looking around, Quinn could see no sign of sleeping mats, just children playing on some big rugs, intricately woven in reds and yellows, and women, who had stopped weaving or embroidering or whatever they were doing, and were staring at Quinn and Zain with wide brown eyes. There was no furniture in the chamber.

"This way," Egunon gestured irritably. He was standing halfway up a set of stairs carved crudely into the rock on the far right-hand side of the chamber and, as Quinn watched, hurried to an arched opening set into the wall and disappeared.

Zain strode across the chamber, with Quinn at his heels, and they soon found themselves in a smaller antechamber, also lit from above through a hole, albeit a smaller one. In here, there was no dazzle, just sacks of rocks lined up in a neat row behind Egunon, who was sitting cross-legged on a thick rug of bright orange. Quinn couldn't help but think that Ash would love to know the secret of that colored dye.

"Sit," said Egunon.

They sat.

"So, the Golden Serpent told you about my stones," Egunon continued. "How much do you know?"

Zain and Quinn exchanged a look, and Quinn wondered what Zain would say.

"It matters not what I know," said Zain, putting on his Hayreddin persona. "All you need to know is that I am here to trade."

Egunon stared at him. "I do not believe you," he said, after a long pause. "It is not food you want, it is my stones."

Quinn was beginning to think that the little man's obsession with rocks was crazy.

Zain shook his head. "No," he said, firmly. "We cannot eat rocks. We want food and then we will be on our way."

"Where are you going?" Egunon asked.

"North," said Zain, shortly.

"Have you come from the south then?" Egunon asked.

Zain frowned. "What is south of here?" he asked, and Quinn sat up straighter. Surely there was nothing beyond this land of sand and caves? The feeling that they were at the edge of the world had not faded, despite the presence of people.

"I do not know for certain," said Egunon, not meeting their eyes, "but I have heard rumors of a land below the horizon."

It was Quinn's turn to frown.

"But they are just rumors," said Egunon, catching sight of Quinn's face.

Then why did you ask if we'd come from there? Quinn thought, opening his mouth to speak.

"Enough small talk," said Zain, throwing a warning glance at him. Quinn got the message: they needed food and these negotiations were already on a knife's edge. "Let us trade."

Egunon leaned back, resting against the sacks behind him. "I think not," he said, with a crafty smile. "Even as we speak, my best men are on their way down to seize your crew members. We shall keep your ship, and everything on it."

Zain sighed as though he'd been expecting this, even as Quinn started in shock. Whatever Egunon had shouted at his men as they'd started down the path, it had put the *Libertas* crew in danger!

"I do not think you want to play it that way," said Zain, quietly.

Quinn shivered at the undercurrent of menace in his voice. Hayreddin was very much back in evidence.

"Ha!" chortled Egunon. "It is already done, and there is nothing you can do to stop it."

"Oh no?" Zain said. He stood, looming over the smaller man, and reached down to grab Egunon by the collar. Egunon struggled, but was no match for Zain's sheer size and strength. "Now you see why I tell you that you must always stay on your feet?" said Zain, conversationally to Quinn, holding the writhing Egunon at arm's length, feet dangling just off the ground.

Quinn nodded.

"As for you," Zain continued, "you're coming with me."

Egunon, his face red with the effort of trying to breathe, couldn't speak, but he flailed his arms wildly and hopelessly in Zain's direction.

Quinn followed his captain as they exited the antechamber and went down the stairs. He could hear a ripple of shocked whispers at their appearance, but nobody rushed forward to try to help Egunon. Instead, they sat in silence as Quinn and Zain walked the width of the chamber, back to where they'd started. Quinn heard a baby cry out, but the sound was quickly muffled.

"Hmm, not too many friends here," Zain said to the wriggling Egunon, as he put the man's feet back on the ground and pushed him through the tunnel, still holding his collar. "Let us see how many you have outside."

Chapter Six

"Quinn!"

He heard Ash's voice before he saw her, blinded as he was by the bright sunshine as he stepped from the tunnel. After a few hard blinks, she swam into view, about six paces away – tied to Tomas and the other Verdanians with thick rope, and being pushed up the cliff path from behind by a line of at least a dozen men holding short, sharp, pointed sticks.

"What we have here," Zain was saying to the men over the heads of the *Libertas* crew, "is a classic impasse. You can not get around us with your prisoners and I –" He paused to lift Egunon slowly from the ground once more, even as the earth beneath their feet began once again to rumble. "I have your leader."

The men did not need to understand Suspite to know what was being said, and their consternation was apparent – though whether that was because of Egunon's plight or the groaning earth, Quinn couldn't be sure. The men waved their sticks threateningly at the Verdanians, one of them jabbing Jericho, who was at the back of the line.

"Hey!" Jericho said, indignantly.

"You could do that," said Zain, thoughtfully. "You could stab all of my crew members . . . Then again . . . I could just do this!"

He swung Egunon to the right, off the path, and dangled him over the long drop down to the beach. The smaller man screamed in terror, and he began shouting at his men in the local language. Quinn noted with interest that there was some crossover with both Barbarin and Deslondic in the sounds of the words, but not enough for him to understand what was being said.

Not that he needed to be fluent in the language to get the drift.

Egunon's men lowered their sticks, and Jericho looked relieved.

"That's better," said Zain. "Much better. Now . . ." He turned to Egunon, feet still kicking over a painful and deadly drop to the beach. "Perhaps you'd like to let my crew go, and begin this discussion again?"

Quinn watched Egunon's face as he battled between anger and resignation, but pragmatism won and he barked a series of orders at his men. They moved, muttering angrily, to untie Jericho, Ash and the others.

Zain held up his left hand to stop them, his right still occupied with the hapless Egunon.

"We'll continue inside, shall we?" Zain growled. "Much more comfortable. Less chance of *accidents*."

Egunon swallowed hard at the last word, as Zain stepped back to allow the *Libertas* crew to enter the tunnel.

"I'll just hold you here until everyone is safely inside," Zain said to Egunon. "Quinn, show Ash the way."

As Quinn led Ash and the others into the darkness, he could hear her voice behind him.

"That was amazing!" she whispered. "I've never seen Zain look so scary."

"Oh, that wasn't Zain," said Quinn, loftily. "That was Hayreddin."

There was a silence. "Looked a lot like Zain to me," she said.

"He was just pretending," said Quinn, uncertainly. "Playing at being a pirate."

Another pause. "I don't know, Quinn," said Ash. "I think he enjoyed that a little bit too much to be acting."

Quinn didn't answer, mulling over her words. It was true that Zain had slipped into the role with ease.

Moments later, all thoughts of Zain left his head as he watched the still-lashed-together *Libertas* crew enter the crystal-studded chamber, enjoying their awestruck expressions at the sparkle of the sunlight on stones.

Tomas, however, outdid them all. Quinn watched as he stumbled forward, dragging with him a very surprised Jericho who was next in line, and fell to his knees, mouth and eyes wide-open, as though struck by magic.

It was not until they were all untied and standing in a huddle, waiting to see what would happen next, that Quinn had a chance to ask Tomas about it.

"They're starstones!" Tomas whispered to Quinn, staring around him. "All of them!"

"Starstones?"

"The rarest and most valuable stone in the world," said Tomas, in awe. "Worth more than gold, much more than your loganstones, more than *anything*."

Staring up at the twinkling stones, which he now noticed seemed to be cut in half and *set* into the chamber walls, Quinn began to wonder about all those men up above, digging, searching, sifting, excited about certain rocks . . . His mind drifted to the sacks lined up in Egunon's chamber, filled with ordinary-looking rocks . . .

"Where do they come from, these starstones?" he asked Tomas.

"Nobody knows," the Barbarin boy replied. "I've only ever seen one before – the Golden Serpent showed it to my father one night when they were drinking *cacao* together."

Thinking quickly, Quinn realized that they had happened upon a starstone mine. Perhaps the only one in the world. Somehow, those boring brown rocks the men were digging up turned into these glowing, glittering kernels of light.

Leaving Tomas, Ash and the others, he moved quickly to follow Zain as he and Egunon once again entered the overseer's small chamber, then stood, shifting from foot to foot, impatiently awaiting a chance to speak, as Zain asked about the seven doors at the other end of the chamber.

"We keep everything there," said Egunon, sulkily. "Food, livestock, other stores."

"All underground?" said Zain. "Why?"

"Out of the heat of the sun and . . ." Egunon seemed to be reaching for the right words in Suspite. "The *killehorn* – rivers of fire."

"Rivers of fire?" burst out Quinn. Zain stopped him with a sharp look.

Egunon smiled strangely. "That rumbling sound you can hear means that they are building. Soon they will overflow, running down the sides of the mountain, across the desert."

"You live under here so they can't get you?" asked Zain.

"Oh, they never reach us here – not quite," said Egunon. "But the air kills everything. The men call it 'dragon's breath' and it dries the eyes, and shrivels the nostrils, burning all the way down to your toes. And so we huddle in here like rats until the rivers stop moving and the dragon's breath is gone."

Quinn shuddered.

"How did you get here?" asked Zain. "Why do you stay?"

"For the stones," said Egunon, in a tone that suggested Zain's mind was feeble. "All of us are here for the stones."

Zain shook his head. "It is no life," he said.

"No," Egunon agreed, sadly, "but we have no choice. All of us – men, women, children – have committed a crime and for that we are sent here to be punished. The only way to repay our debt to the chieftains is to send the stones."

Quinn had a sudden picture in his mind of the jubilation of the men above when rocks had stuck to the pig fat. "*One step closer to home,*" Egunon had said.

"Where are the chieftains now?" asked Zain, frowning.

"To the east," Egunon responded, waving vaguely behind him.

"And they trust you to trade for them?" Zain's expression was skeptical. "With anyone who sails past?"

"We all do the best we can," said Egunon, smile once again crafty, and Quinn knew that the chieftains in the east knew nothing of Egunon's dealings with pirates.

"Very well," sighed Zain, "let us begin."

Quinn stood still and silent as time ticked away and the two men haggled over food supplies, with Zain trying to make the few gold coins he had left go as far as possible. Even the ever-increasing creaking and groaning of the walls around them did not hurry them. Eventually, the discussion began to wind down and he could see them preparing to spit on their hands to seal the deal.

"We'll take a sack of your stones, as well," Quinn interrupted, before they could shake on it.

Zain turned to him, eyebrow raised as a shower of dust rained down on him.

"Just one sack," Quinn said, putting on his most trustworthy face. He didn't have time to explain everything to Zain now. Besides, he wasn't entirely sure his theory was even correct – and he really wanted a chance to find out.

Still looking quizzical, Zain turned back to Egunon. "One sack of rocks it is," he said.

But Egunon was shaking his head. "No, no, no," he said. "They are not part of the deal."

Zain looked at Quinn. "Do we really want them?" he asked in Verdanian so that Egunon could not follow the conversation. "A sack of rocks? I get the feeling that we need to get out of here." His words were punctuated by another fall of rocks. Egunon frowned.

"We do," said Quinn, firmly. "They will help with the treasure component of our race."

The race around the world was about bringing back the best and most beautiful map within a year, but additional treasure would be looked upon favorably.

"We have the loganstones for that," said Zain. "And we have completed the deal. We have what we need."

"We need those," said Quinn, clutching for a reason that would convince him, even as the ground began to shake beneath his feet. "The others will not have them."

"No, Odilon and Dolan will probably not present the King with a sack of rocks," agreed Zain, raising his voice above the din.

"Trust me," shouted Quinn, brushing dirt from his hair. "Did you see how Tomas reacted to this cave?"

When they'd left him in the main cave, Tomas was still reeling at the sight of so many starstones in one place. Somehow, Quinn knew, those rocks became starstones – why else would Egunon's invisible masters in the east be pulling them out of the ground? Quinn just needed to get his hands on the stones and work out how to make them shine.

Zain nodded, then composed his face into a menacing scowl, and turned back to Egunon, who quailed as Hayreddin emerged once more. "Perhaps you and I should go outside and discuss this some more?" Zain asked, stepping towards Egunon, hand outstretched. "After all, they're only rocks."

"No!" shouted Egunon, throwing his hands in the air in surrender. The thought of going outside seemed to terrify him. "Take them and go. Just . . . go!"

Zain didn't need telling again. Quinn followed him, dragging the sack, as he strode from the antechamber into the main cave . . . and chaos. Ash, Tomas and the others were standing, openmouthed, in a huddle as women and children ran screaming around them. The very walls around them were shaking, and great cracks had begun to appear under the sparkling rocks in the wall.

"What's happening?" shouted Quinn.

"It is the mountain," said Egunon from the doorway of his antechamber. "The mountain is angry. The *killehorn* will be flowing down her sides."

Quinn gasped. "But it won't reach us here – you said so! So why are they screaming?"

"It has not reached us yet," said Egunon again, with that same strange smile. "But each time it draws closer . . ."

By now, Zain had reached the *Libertas* crew and they were scrambling to gather the pile of supplies put aside for them, before ducking, one by one, back into the dark tunnel that led to the outside world.

Swallowing hard, Quinn followed, stepping into the blackness, trying not to fall too far behind. As he struggled to drag the sack through the soft sand of the tunnel, the walls around him continued to creak, and he felt as though they were pressing closer and closer. He concentrated on breathing, putting one foot in front of the other, listening for Zain and the others above the groaning agony of the rock.

He heard a shout ahead, and pulled at the sack even harder, rounding the last bend to find a line of *Libertas* crew ahead of him.

"What's the holdup?" he asked Tomas, his frame discernible in the shadows by the halo of curls backlit by the light of the tunnel opening.

"It's raining fire," his friend answered, sounding dazed. "Look!"

Dropping the sack, Quinn pushed past Tomas for a better look and found to his amazement that his friend was right. Tiny drops of fire were sprinkling down the mouth of the tunnel.

"Forward!" roared Zain. "Get out of here as fast as you can!"

"Through that?" questioned Quinn, disbelieving.

"You heard what the man said in there," shouted Zain. "*Rivers* of fire! These are droplets – but if we don't get out of here *now*, there may well be a deluge!"

Quinn gulped. The rest of the crew were moving, grasping their boxes and bags tightly and, looking neither right nor left, hurtling through the tunnel opening. Quinn had no choice but to grab his sack and follow.

Outside, the air was stale, and he had to take shallow breaths to breathe at all. Looking ahead, he could see that Ash had drawn the top of her tunic up over her nose and mouth, and he quickly did the same. The smell wasn't much better inside his tunic, although at least the thick cotton seemed to stop the terrible burning in his throat and nose. Black soot made his eyes stream, but there wasn't much he could do about that.

Quinn heard a short howl of pain, and saw Ison brushing madly at his forearm. The sailor habitually wore his sleeves rolled up, and it seemed one of the drops of fire had landed on this skin. Quinn tucked his own sleeves over his fingers, covering as much as he could. It made dragging the sack awkward, but at least he was protected.

As Quinn struggled down another ladder, swearing and cursing, Jericho waited at the bottom, laughing up at him. "Planning to use those rocks to build up muscles," he jibed.

"Something like that," Quinn muttered, hoping that his gamble was going to pay off and that all this effort was going to be worth it.

When at last he reached the beach, Quinn flopped on the sand, panting. Down here at the bottom of the cliff, the air was a little clearer, helped along by the sea breeze.

"Don't get too comfortable," Zain ordered. "Look up there!"

Quinn opened his eyes to stare at the cliff top above him – and was quickly on his feet, sack in hand. "What *is* that?"

To their right, a long, slow snake of red was curling towards the cliff's edge, seeping slowly but surely over the top.

"The *killehorn*," answered Zain, quietly.

"But Egunon said . . ."

"It seems that Egunon was wrong."

"We have to get out of here!" said Quinn.

"Indeed," said Zain, turning towards the beach and the longboat. "Indeed we do."

They ran as fast as they could towards the boat, choking and spluttering as the air grew fouler around them. Once in the boat, Jericho and Ison took the oars and rowed with all their might towards the *Libertas*.

Quinn, Tomas and Ash watched in horror as the sand goblins swarmed down the cliffs to the safety of the beach. Even as they ran for the water, Quinn could see the rivers of fire cascade over the clifftop, like burning waterfalls, before slowing into black sludge on the sand.

The sand goblins stood in the water and watched.

"Do you think they'll be all right?" asked Ash.

Quinn shuddered. "I don't know," he admitted. "I think the ones in the water are okay – and those who stayed in the cave will be protected . . ." His mind refused to think about that open square that allowed light to pour in. His skin prickled with goose pimples as he thought of what those rivers of fire might do to anyone caught in their path.

Back on board the *Libertas*, he stood at the rail and took in the whole scene from the height of the deck. He could see the menacing mountain still belching in the background, though the rivers of fire had slowed and seemed to have hardened in places.

As Quinn watched, he could see that some of the sand

goblins were picking their way back up the cliff, back to their daily grind of dragging stones out of the desert.

The sight brought Quinn back to the thought of his own stones. Eager as he was to test his theory about the "rocks" in his sack, he first helped store the supplies and get the ship underway – anything to get as far away from this tainted shore as possible.

Once that was done, however, he went in search of Ash – it was time to test his idea about the rocks and their secrets, despite his empty stomach.

"Can I borrow your knife?" he asked Ash. It was hard to believe that he'd been at sea for more than eight months, had traveled countless miles, and still was not in possession of a knife of his own.

"If you'll help me carry these down to the cleric," she replied, indicating the bowls of food she'd conjured up within moments of being back on deck. "I'm not sure what he'll be able to eat, he's so weak, but I thought I'd try a bit of everything to tempt him."

Looking at the selection, Quinn's stomach growled. "Sure," he said, putting his sack on the deck next to the wheelhouse, deciding that his stomach probably couldn't wait until after his rock experiment after all. "I've been meaning to ask why you ended up on the beach." Against Zain's express wishes, he finished silently.

Juggling three bowls, she looked sheepish. "Well, the cleric told me I should go," she said. "I was really mad at being left behind and, you know what he's like, such an old dear. He told me he'd be fine and that I should go and find him something good to eat and leave him in peace for a few moments."

"What are those?" Quinn asked, indicating three small packets she'd tucked into the side of a bowl of what looked like dried peas.

"Oh, one of the women gave them to me while you and Zain were busy trading with that funny little man," said Ash with a bemused smile. "She was cooking and I wandered over for a look. They're ground powders, and she was sprinkling them in the food. I was hoping the cleric could help me work out what they are. They all smell earthy, but different – and that one is really hot!" She nodded with her head to indicate the packet nearest her arm.

"Maybe they're poisonous?" Quinn said in alarm.

"Given that she was sprinkling them on their meal, I doubt it." With that she turned on her heel and he could only follow her down the stairs, trying to balance his own bowls, muttering under his breath.

Back on deck, delivery made and Ash's knife in his hand, Quinn bolted down a large bowl of the same peas they'd taken to the cleric, which were surprisingly delicious and, joy of joys, three strips of dried meat, tough and chewy and the best thing he'd tasted in months.

Sated, he turned his attention to the sack – it looked to be less full than he remembered.

"Cleaver?" he asked the first mate, who was in the wheelhouse steering the *Libertas* away from shore. "Have you seen anyone hanging around here?"

"Near your pile of old rocks, you mean?" teased Cleaver, puffing on his ever-present pipe.

"Yes," said Quinn impatiently.

"Nope, just you. Not too many of us interested in lumps of dirt."

Quinn rolled his eyes and slid down the wall beside the sack. He was sure it contained fewer rocks than he'd carried on board but, then again, his mind could be playing tricks on him. He sighed, hating the uncertainty that the holes in his memory brought him.

Pulling out a rock, he examined it closely. The surface felt oily under his fingers, but as he brushed at it, the dirty exterior gave way to . . . a dirty interior. Disappointed, Quinn peered at it more closely. He'd been hoping to see the sparkle and shine of the starstones he'd seen in the chamber, but there was no sign.

He turned the rock this way and that, noting its rounded shape. Taking Ash's knife, he tried to etch a thin line across the top of the rock, but was surprised when the blade didn't even scratch the surface.

Quinn frowned.

Turning the blade point down, he put the rock on the deck at his feet and thrust down at it again and again. The blade merely bounced off.

Leif's boots! Beginning to sweat as the late-afternoon sun beat down on him and his frantic efforts produced nothing, Quinn began to think he'd gotten it all wrong. He'd been so sure that he would open the sack, dust off some dirt and produce a small mountain of starstones, making him a hero! Instead, it seemed as though the crew was right to laugh at his "old rocks."

"You might need to try more force," said Tomas, standing over Quinn.

"What do you mean?" Quinn asked, pushing his sweaty hair out of his eyes to look up at his friend.

"Starstones are meant to be really hard," said Tomas, taking Quinn by surprise. "What?" Tomas continued. "I'm not silly – I mention starstones and you're suddenly desperate for a sack of old rocks. Seems to me there's a link . . ."

Quinn said nothing.

"Anyway, the legend says that they fell from up there." Tomas pointed upward. "If they came all the way down from the sky without shattering, they must be tough. The Golden Serpent told my father that you could etch gold with them."

Quinn looked at the rock in his hand, considering. "Can you go and ask Ison for that mallet he uses when he's doing the ship repairs?" he asked.

As Tomas hurried off, Quinn put the rock down on the deck, and positioned the knife, point down, vertical at its center.

"What are you going to do?" asked Tomas when he returned.

"I'm not sure," admitted Quinn, "But I'm willing to try everything." He tapped hard at the knife handle. Nothing. Lifting the mallet, he brought it down with more force. Nothing.

"Maybe try moving the point more to one side," suggested Tomas. "It's thickest in the center. You might have more luck on the edges."

Quinn nodded, shifting his knife point. This time, when he lifted the mallet, he bashed down as hard as he could, reeling back in surprise when the rock suddenly sheared in two, sending the halves skittering across the deck, and the knife point buried itself in the deck, just a hand span from his boot.

Ignoring the close call, he crawled across the deck after one of the halves – turning it over in his hand to reveal a plane of translucent, glittering crystal.

"Quinn!" said Tomas excitedly, picking up the other half. "You've discovered a starstone!"

"Not just one," said Quinn triumphantly. "I've got a whole sackful of those 'old rocks!'"

The two boys looked at each other, threw their heads back and laughed.

Chapter Seven

Later that night, his belly full, Quinn lolled on the deck of the *Libertas*, staring up at the thick carpet of stars strewn across the sky. Ostensibly, he was working, charting the positions of the sparkling jewels above him, but really he was soaking up the peace and contentment he felt while gazing at the heavens. When the stars were shining, he felt closer to home, able to imagine that if he just followed their bright path, he'd soon be back with his family.

He remembered those dark weeks aboard the *Black Hawk* when he'd spent so much time locked up in the hold, and shuddered.

The stars were a constant in his shifting world, and he liked to know they were there. Even if, he acknowledged, their patterns had changed so much over the past few months as to become unrecognizable. So much so that Quinn had started a chart, quite separate to his maps (fake and real), of the layout of the stars.

"We call that one the Dog," said Tomas, rolling over to point at Quinn's chart. "See – four legs, tail, nose." He indicated the vague outline of a dog, before returning to his original position – flat on his back beside Quinn.

Quinn laughed. "I see it!" he said, making a note of the name. "Any others?"

"Of course," said Tomas, lazily. "We have names for all of them."

Quinn looked up, unable to even imagine the number of stars overhead. "All of them?" he quizzed.

"Well," said Tomas, following his gaze. "The biggest and brightest. The ones that wink and shout to be noticed."

"You certainly showed a good eye for that today," said Quinn, as Tomas made himself comfortable, arm under his head.

Tomas laughed. "It was hard to miss when you knew what you were looking at," he said. "A little bit like Ash."

Both boys laughed again. Having managed to live on board the *Libertas* for months as a boy, Ash had been unmasked as a girl by Tomas within days of his arrival. Quinn sobered when he remembered the consequences of that and the vote that Ash had told him about when he'd returned from the *Black Hawk* – she'd had to watch while the rest of the crew decided whether she was to stay aboard the *Libertas* and live, or go over the side and die.

"I think she's proven that girls are not bad luck on ships," said Quinn.

Tomas looked at him. "I'm not sure the crew would agree, from what I've heard. She was most recently blamed for the lack of food."

Quinn sighed. "It wasn't like she ate it all," he muttered.

"Everything that goes wrong will be her fault until we dock in – where *are* we going to dock anyway?" asked Tomas.

"Oakston, capital of Verdania," said Quinn.

Tomas stretched out on his back. "Home," he said flatly. "Strange to be going 'home' to a place you've only heard about."

Quinn looked across at his friend. "Do you miss Barbarin?" he asked, already knowing the answer. Wasn't he still missing his home, eight months after leaving it, and knowing that he would be returning? *Should* be returning, he amended, crossing his fingers. Who was he to say that they were even now traveling in the direction of home? With two-thirds of their year-long quest over, Zain had ordered that they head north once they'd reached this strange, dead land, but that was more a matter of hope than knowledge.

All they knew was that heading farther south was probably the wrong direction. Maybe.

"I miss it every day," said Tomas, his voice fierce. "One minute I hate my father for sending me here, the next I miss him so much I could cry. Zain tells me that I'll probably feel that way for the rest of my life. Even if I love

Verdania." He turned to face Quinn, eyes wide. "I don't even know where I'm going to live, Quinn. My father had family in a place called Tumdurran, but he didn't know if any of them were still alive. And none of them will know me."

Given that Tomas's father was one of Verdania's most wanted thieves, Quinn couldn't help but think that Tumdurran might not be the best place for Tomas.

"Zain will look after you," he said with more confidence than he felt. Zain lived in the palace, with a wife and a daughter, at the beck and call of the King. If they won the race, however, and Zain regained his freedom, he might even want to return to Deslond . . . Quinn felt sad at that thought.

"I'm not sure he'll be able to," said Tomas. "And that wasn't part of the deal. Father paid him to get me to Verdania, no more."

"Well, you'll have to come home with me then," said Quinn, surprising himself with the offer. He wondered how his da and mam, already dealing with six boys in a small cottage, would react if he brought home another one.

"Won't you have Ash?" asked Tomas, who knew that Ash was on her own.

"She'll never go back to Markham," Quinn said sadly. "I don't *even* have to ask her. I don't know what she'll want to do when we return."

It was strange to be talking about returning while they were still out here, surrounded by leagues and leagues of curling waves. Quinn thought back to the early days of this race, when the only question on his lips was not "when" they would return, but "if." Then, he would have done anything to get back home, because the world was so scary and every day was a new challenge. Now, he realized, going back home was going to bring its own challenges.

But not for him, he thought. He knew where he was going. He knew that his map was clear and accurate and beautiful. All they had to do was to get back to Verdania first.

Quinn frowned at the thought. There had been no sign of the other two explorers' ships. The *Wandering Spirit* and the *Fair Maiden* had disappeared after docking in Barbarin. Just thinking about that last meeting made Quinn's fists clench. Odilon had made a deal with Juan Forden, handing Quinn and, he'd thought, Ira, over in an attempt to get the winning edge in the race around the world.

Ira had escaped at Quinn's expense – and Quinn's anger rose as he thought of how Ira had pushed him into a dark pit, leaving him to be dragged aboard the Gelynion's ship and forced to work for them.

Wherever it was, their next meeting was going to be an interesting one if Quinn had anything to do with it.

Then again, for all he knew, Dolan and Ira and Odilon and Ajax were either all lost at sea forever – he had a sudden pleasing vision of the *Wandering Spirit* disappearing under black waves – or all back at home in Verdania right now, drinking honeyed tea with Queen Lorelei and crowing about how they'd known that a slave and a farm boy should never have been allowed to compete in the Great Race in the first place.

Not that Ajax would take part in *that* conversation. Having lived aboard the *Libertas* for several weeks he had, Quinn knew, a healthy respect for Zain and his crew.

"I'm going to bed," said Tomas, interrupting Quinn's thoughts with a huge yawn.

"You go ahead," said Quinn, wanting some time alone to recapture his earlier feeling of peace. "I'll be down in a minute. I'm just going to enjoy the clearer air a bit longer." Now that hunger was no longer a problem, the *Libertas* was back under full sail and Cleaver had taken her far enough off the coastline to avoid the bitter tang in the air. The mountain with its halo of smoke was still visible behind them, but growing rapidly smaller.

Tomas had been gone only a moment or two before a shadow detached itself from the wall behind the wheelhouse.

Quinn didn't even have to look up to know who it was, though he turned to face the threat. "Kurt," he said evenly in Suspite. "Still snooping and sniveling in the dark, I see."

Kurt's sneer was clear, even in the moonlight. "You think you're so smart," he replied. "But I know better than that."

Quinn forced a laugh, wincing when the effort brought a burning pain to his head. "What is it that you think you know?"

Kurt tapped his forehead. "I know that things in here are not as they should be," he said. "I watch, and I know."

Quinn tried to remain calm, reminding himself that there was no way Kurt could know about the holes in his memory. He was, as usual, trying to cause Quinn trouble. "You're always hiding in corners, creeping around, turning up where you shouldn't. But that doesn't mean you know anything . . . Besides . . ." He rolled away from Kurt with an exaggerated calm. "Nobody listens to you anyway."

He could almost hear Kurt seething behind him – he wanted more than anything to take Quinn's role as mapmaker. But Quinn knew that while *he* was on board the *Libertas*, nobody paid any attention to Kurt. Which drove Kurt mad.

As Kurt stomped away, Quinn lay on deck, eyes wide, wondering. What had Kurt seen that had given him the confidence to even make that remark about his memory?

It was a question that would keep Quinn awake for a very long time that night.

Chapter Eight

Rubbing his tired eyes, Quinn stared at the wooden chips in front of him.

"Come on, make a move," said Jericho, stroking his moustache with such glee that Quinn knew he was about to be beaten.

"Oh well," he sighed, throwing out a chip marked with three triangles. "It's only a game."

"Ha!" chortled Jericho, placing a chip with five triangles on top. "I win!"

Quinn gathered his remaining chips together and handed them over, smiling through his frustration. When he'd first begun to learn this game, he'd had a winning streak that lasted for weeks – mostly because he'd realized he could keep track of all the chips in the game by remembering what each player had already put down. The aim of the game was to be the last player to put a chip down before the total tally got to forty-two. If your chip took the score over forty-two, you lost, so the object was to get as close to the mark as you could.

The trouble was, he was now struggling to remember what his opponents had thrown out into the mix, and what they might have in their hands.

"Again?" said Jericho.

Abel and Dilly nodded.

"I'm out," said Quinn.

"You're off your game," said Jericho. "Sure you don't want to practice?"

Quinn laughed. "Take more chores off you, you mean?"

The winner of each game won the right to allocate one of his daily tasks to the loser of his choice. So far, Quinn was doing Jericho's early morning watch duty for the next three days.

"Well, if you put it like that . . ." Jericho's smile was pure mischief.

"Sorry," said Quinn, shaking his head. "Find another mark."

Before he'd even begun playing the game with the crew, Cleaver had told Quinn that Jericho was the man to watch. "He used to play down at the docks, using it as a way to get money for food . . . he won't hold back."

Still, Quinn had held his own, losing just enough hands to ensure the rest of the crew wouldn't ban him from playing. But not anymore.

He stepped back from the playing circle, allowing Cook, who'd finished his breakfast chores, to take his place. Turning, he almost stepped on Kurt, who liked to hang around the games, even though he never played.

Kurt smirked.

Quinn opened his mouth to speak to him, but closed it just as quickly. He had better things to do than argue with Kurt – but he now had an idea of what had prompted Kurt's remarks of the night before. If he'd been watching Quinn play closely, he'd know that he wasn't winning like he used to . . .

"Quinn! Quinn!"

He turned his back on Kurt as Ash rushed towards him.

"It's the cleric," she said, her blue eyes full of worry. "He wants to see you." She led the way to the stairs.

"How is he today?"

"A little better," she said. "He can't seem to get enough of that green soup Cook made him."

Knowing that the small supply of fresh vegetables they'd bought from Egunon wouldn't last long, Cook had decided to blend them all into a broth to stretch them out. In his weakened state, the cleric couldn't eat much else.

"Well, you've always said that greens are good for us," said Quinn, wrinkling his nose. He didn't mind a few vegetables with his meals, but he really didn't like peas. Or broccoli. Or spinach. Or . . . it was quite a long list, he realized.

"I'm beginning to think that they hold the key to the cleric's illness," she said. "There's something in them that his body can't do without."

"Well, if he needs them that badly, then he should have mine as well," said Quinn generously.

Ash laughed. "Nice try, Quinn – if his body needs them, then so does yours. The only reason we're not really sick too is that we're younger, so we don't notice the effects as much."

Sometimes he wished his friend didn't know quite so much about plants and healing . . .

"I'll leave you here," she said, at the door of Quinn's own cabin. "I want to talk to Tomas about those powders we got from Egunon. He thinks they may come from seeds or pods."

With that, she was gone, leaving Quinn to continue alone. Pushing open the door to the cleric's cabin, Quinn squinted as his eyes adjusted to the gloom. The curtains were pulled tight over the porthole, and the air was stuffy.

"Cleric?"

"Ah, Quinn," came a quavering voice from the bed, which was built into the wall, like Quinn's. "Good to see you."

"And you," said Quinn, trying to hide his shock as he took in the cleric's appearance. He was lying back against his pillows, gaunt and pale. His body seemed tiny under the brown woolen blanket.

"I wanted to make sure you were not missing your map," said the cleric. "I know that you must be itching to work on it."

Quinn had not been down for several days, in deference to the cleric's condition. "I'm okay," he said. In truth, however, he was worried. He knew that his memory was unreliable and he needed to record his thoughts. Over the past few days, he'd taken the precaution of putting true calculations and information onto the fake map, much as it pained him to do so.

"Do it now," the cleric said. "Sit with me a while and tell me what you're seeing."

Quinn looked around uncertainly. It really was dim in the cabin.

"Oh, pull back those curtains," the cleric said. "I have been in the dark for too long."

And so Quinn sat at the cleric's worn, wooden desk, and updated his map as best he could, while telling the cleric of the adventures over the past few days.

"Starstones, you say," said the cleric. "I have read about those in books, but always imagined them to be mythical."

"I'll bring one down to show you," Quinn promised, brow wrinkled as he tried to remember the exact line of the coast around Egunon's mine. He sighed. It was no good. He was going to have to refer to the fake map.

"Quinn," the cleric said, and his serious tone had Quinn putting down his quill and turning back to face the figure in the bed. "If anything should happen to me . . ." He held up a hand to still Quinn's fervent protests. "If anything should happen to me," he continued, serenely, "make sure the King gets my letters."

Quinn smiled. The cleric had been busily writing letters to the King ever since the *Libertas* had set sail from Verdania. Everyone on board had humored his efforts, despite the fact that there was nowhere to mail them.

"I will," Quinn said now. "But nothing will happen."

It was the cleric's turn to smile. "The confidence of youth," he said. "I –"

"Ship! Ship ahoy!"

Whatever Cleric Greenfield had been about to say was suddenly lost as Ison's voice echoed around the *Libertas*.

"A ship!" exclaimed Quinn. "I wonder if it's the *Fair Maiden*."

While Quinn would be happy never to see Odilon of Blenheim, captain of that ship, ever again, the idea of seeing Ajax had him on his feet in excitement.

"There's only one way to find out," said the cleric. "Go ahead."

Quinn rolled his map up and slid it back into its hiding place in the secret pocket in the cleric's simple cotton curtains.

"Will you come?" he asked, as he hurried towards the door.

"Perhaps," said the cleric. "I might wait to hear who it is before I make the effort." His tone of voice suggested that even the all-forgiving cleric had a blacklist these days.

～

"That's not a Verdanian ship."

Arriving up on deck, Quinn had found the entire crew lined up on the port side of the *Libertas*, staring at the long, low ship that lay about a league ahead of them. It was rigged with just one huge square sail.

"No," said Zain, standing beside him. "No, Quinn Freeman, that is a Deslondic dragon boat."

Deslondic?

"But that means . . ."

"Yes," said Zain, his eyes never leaving the boat. "It means that we are either approaching Deslond from the south – or that dragon boat is a long way from home."

As Quinn watched the boat, he tried to think what this might signify for the *Libertas* – but mostly what it might mean for Zain and the other Deslonders aboard. He became aware that the dragon boat was behaving very strangely – and heading in the direction of the *Libertas*.

"Zain, what are they doing?" he asked, watching the way the boat would rush forward, and then stop, then rush forward again. As it came closer, he could see its unusual prow, which arched up towards the sky.

"I think they are . . . chasing something," Zain replied.

"They may be fishing?" ventured Jericho.

There was silence as all on board the *Libertas* watched the dragon boat.

"They are fishing . . ." said Quinn slowly, eyes on the water ahead of the strange ship, "but for what?"

Even as the words left his mouth, a white shape reared up out of the water ahead of them.

"Quinn!" shouted Ash. "It's Nammu."

Nammu was the name Quinn had given the mysterious sea creature who had accompanied their journey around the world, appearing and disappearing at different times. The other crew members simply referred to her as a "monster," but Quinn was convinced the creature was good luck.

Although . . .

"No!" he responded, shaking his head, as the shape in front of them disappeared back into the waves. "That is too small to be Nammu. Unless . . ."

His unspoken question was answered moments later when a huge white tail suddenly appeared from beneath the waves, hurtling towards the sky before slapping back onto the water with a resounding crack, sending waves roaring back towards the dragon boat.

As the boat tossed and turned in the angry water, Quinn smiled. "That was Nammu," he said. "The other must be her baby."

"Baby?" Cleaver said. "That thing was *huge*."

But Quinn had no time for jokes. "Zain, we have to help her," he said. "The dragon boat is trying to catch her baby. We have to stop them!"

Zain looked down at him. "You want me to sail between a Deslondic dragon boat and its quarry?"

"YES!" screamed Quinn, watching in horror as the dragon boat recovered its forward motion and began relentlessly pursuing the smaller white beast again. Even as he watched, the younger creature seemed to tire, lolling on top of the water, visible to the eye – and vulnerable to capture.

Quinn clutched Zain's sleeve. "We have to help them," he repeated. "Nammu saved us, Zain. We owe her."

Zain gave him a long look. "So you say," he said.

But Jericho was shaking his head. "You know the law of the sea, Zain. That *thing* belongs to them. If we interfere, we'll be in trouble."

Quinn banged his hand against the rail. "If we don't save them, then we'll be in bigger trouble," he said. "All our luck will go."

"Can I help?" said a frail voice behind them.

Zain and Quinn turned to face Cleric Greenfield, who was standing behind them, his brown robe flapping in the stiff breeze.

"It is good to see you up and about," said Zain, taking the cleric by the arm and leading him, on unsteady feet, to the rail. "Quinn wishes me to start a fight to save his Nammu."

Cleric Greenfield nodded, staring at the scene unfolding before them. "I see."

"I just wonder whether a fight is worth it," said Zain.

"A fight is always worth it when it is on the side of right," said the cleric.

"But in a fight, everyone is always convinced they are right," replied Zain. "Nobody goes into a fight because they think they are wrong."

Cleric Greenfield smiled. "Of course," he said. "But you will know what to do, Zain."

"Can we stop talking about this and *do something?*" interrupted Quinn in frustration. The dragon boat had now sailed between Nammu's young one, which was swimming in circles in agitation, and the great rippling circle of bubbles that marked Nammu's last position. Quinn watched, desperately hoping the great white creature would simply rise up under the dragon boat and blow them out of the water.

"Where is she?" he breathed.

"Dragon boats are fast and agile," said Zain, as the smaller boat zipped closer to the baby, "which makes them valuable in battles. It's unusual to see one used for fishing."

Even as he spoke, Nammu rose up out of the water, but Quinn could see that she had been confused by the speed of the dragon boat and had misjudged her reentry.

"She's come up on the wrong side of them!" he said. "Zain, we have to help!"

The dragon boat crew was now throwing long ropes with large, wicked hooks attached to the end towards the younger creature, who quickly became tangled, the water turning red around it as the hooks pierced its white skin. Panicked and confused, Nammu was too far away to assist.

"Very well, Quinn Freeman," said Zain. "We will take a run at this, but we will not do it because of your 'luck.' We will do it because that baby cannot fend for itself."

Jericho and Cleaver shook their heads doubtfully. "They won't like it," said Cleaver.

"No," said Zain. "They will not. Hoist all the sails."

As the crew ran to do Zain's bidding and the *Libertas* picked up speed and changed direction to sail at the dragon boat, Quinn moved to the bow so that he could see what was happening. The Deslondic boat stayed at a distance from the baby, giving it slack while keeping it tangled up. If they got too close, they would be pulled into the maelstrom that the thrashing creature was creating, so they seemed content to wait until it tired.

As the *Libertas* drew nearer, Quinn could see that the dragon boat carried a surprising number of men. Half a dozen were clinging desperately to the long ropes wrapped around the baby, while another six or seven stood nearby, clutching long, pointed sticks.

Quinn rushed to the wheelhouse, where Zain had taken control of the ship as Ash watched on.

"What are you going to do?" Quinn asked.

"As I see it," said Zain, "the only thing we can do is to get between that dragon boat and the creature – and hope that your Nammu does not decide to take us all out."

Nammu was now circling the scene, using her huge tail to create wave after wave to rock the dragon boat. But the light ship was designed to skate the surface of such waves, and its high prow cut a path through those that did break over it.

"Why doesn't the baby dive?" asked Ash. "They'd have to let go then."

"It may be too young to know that it *can* dive," Zain answered. "It was not with Nammu when last we saw her, and that was just a few weeks ago." He looked back to the horizon, face suddenly grim. "Grab hold of something!" he shouted.

Quinn and Ash clutched at the wheelhouse door frame, turning just in time to see the *Libertas* sail within an arm's length of the dragon boat. Zain had steered them into the narrow space between the boat and the creature. The *Libertas* shuddered and stalled briefly as the ropes caught around her bow, but then they were free and moving at speed through the water. The dragon boat crew had simply dropped the ropes, realizing they couldn't contain the bigger ship.

Racing to the stern, Quinn and Ash cheered as Nammu swam over their wake to nudge her bleeding baby, diving down into the depths and taking it with her. Ropes floated to the surface, and Quinn could only hope that there were not too many of those wicked hooks in the baby's flesh.

"We did it!" said Ash, eyes shining.

"We sure did," said Tomas, but he was not looking at the spot where Nammu had disappeared. Rather, he was staring to port side, his mouth open in shock and disbelief.

Quinn turned to follow his gaze, his own stomach dropping to his feet. Swarming over the port rail was a group of huge, angry Deslonders, their faces twisted in rage! In that instant, Quinn could see Zain's point about not wanting to start a fight . . .

"Don't just stand there!" Tomas shouted, bringing Quinn to his senses. "Grab a weapon!"

A roar sounded from the wheelhouse, and suddenly Zain was at the rail, his huge two-handed sword swinging over his head. Jericho and Ison were close behind, brandishing their own weapons. Dilly dropped down from the mast, a knife between his teeth, while Abel and Cook ran from the galley.

At the sight of them, the leading Deslonders paused – but not for long. With a howl, they threw themselves onto the deck, thrusting their long, pointed sticks at the *Libertas* crew.

Stunned, Quinn watched helplessly as more and more Deslonders streamed over the rail. The *Libertas* crew was fighting bravely, but were hopelessly outnumbered.

"Come on, Quinn," said Ash, pulling her knife from her boot. "We have to help!"

Grabbing Ison's mallet, which was propped nearby, Quinn followed his friend into the fray, with Tomas at his heels.

"Trip them!" Quinn shouted at Tomas, realizing that the best thing that he and his friends could do against the oversized Deslonders was to create a nuisance. And so he and Ash and Tomas ran headlong at the fighting Deslonders, using roundhouse kicks to take their feet out from under them wherever they could.

The tactic seemed to be working, and the tide of the battle was evening out when Quinn was startled by a sharp, twanging noise. Looking up, he saw a storm of arrows raining down on the deck.

"They're shooting at us!" shouted Ash. "What can we do?"

"Over here!" screamed Tomas, beckoning from the rail. "The archer is in the boat!"

Rushing to the rail, Quinn saw that his friend was right. A lone archer was standing in the safety of the dragon boat, shooting arrow after arrow up and over the rail.

"We need to get down there!" he shouted. "We have to –"

Whatever he was about to say was lost as a great bellow of pain sounded across the deck. Quinn had only ever heard a sound like that once before, and it was when his da's biggest bull had been gored in a fight with a neighbor's even larger bull. Hardly daring to look, he turned from the rail to see Zain crashing to the deck like a falling oak, an arrow in his left shoulder, blood gushing down his arm.

"No!" screamed Ash, thrusting her knife handle at Quinn, and darting towards the captain. She reached Zain's side just as a Deslonder did, throwing herself across Zain's fallen body.

"You're not having him!" she screamed in fury at the Deslonder, who seemed so startled by her act that he stood, uncertainly, sword in hand.

"Get away!" said Quinn to the Deslonder as he reached Zain, with Tomas by his side. Both boys held their knives in front of them, ready to defend their captain.

Bemused, the Deslonder stared at them.

"Go!" said Quinn, advancing on the Deslonder, heart in his mouth, knife poised, Tomas beside him.

The Deslonder looked down at Zain, whose blood was now seeping across the deck.

"Bah!" he said in Deslondic, striding away to rejoin the fight. "He won't last. You can have him!"

"What did he say?" shouted Tomas breathlessly, still waving his knife.

"I don't think he gives Zain much hope," said Quinn, lowering his knife and turning back to Ash, who was working feverishly on Zain, muttering to herself.

Quinn dropped down beside her. "What do I need to do?" he asked Ash, yelling to be heard over the noise of the battle.

"Help me get the arrow out," she said, close to his ear.

"I thought you were meant to leave it in," said Quinn, worriedly. He had a vague memory of his da talking about this after a friend of his had been hurt in a hunting accident. He had never wished more that he could remember *exactly* what his da had said that night.

"I don't think that will help here," Ash said. "The quicker we can get it out, the quicker we can stop the bleeding."

"But won't it just bleed more?" asked Tomas, also squatting beside them.

Ash looked at him. "Probably," she said, "which is why you need to take off your shirt. You too, Quinn."

Both boys stripped their shirts over their heads and held them, ready.

"Right," said Ash. "Hold him down, Quinn. Tomas, give me your knife."

Quinn thanked all the gods that Zain was still unconscious. If he hadn't been, Quinn could sit on him and still not "hold him down."

Working quickly, Ash made four short but deep cuts around the arrowhead.

Zain flinched, but did not move.

"Right," said Ash, "now we just pull it out."

She took a deep breath and Quinn could see she was steeling herself.

"I'll do it," he said, wanting to take some of the responsibility from her. She nodded her agreement. He reached forward, grasped the arrow at the base and pulled straight up, as hard as he could. With a ripping, squelching sound, the arrow came free – and a fountain of blood appeared.

"Ash!" Quinn shouted in panic.

Ash now stuffed as much of Quinn's shirt into the wound as she could, and folded Tomas's red shirt across the top, forming a thick pad, and then leaned on the wound with as much pressure as possible.

Quinn watched, unable to believe that Zain remained, to all intents and purposes, "asleep."

"I'll get Cleaver," said Tomas, watching as blood began to bloom, darkening the bright red of the fabric to deep claret, soaking halfway up the pad.

"He's busy," said Ash. "It will be okay. Get a blanket instead."

"A blanket?" said Tomas. "It's boiling hot!"

"My mam always covered people in a blanket," said Ash. "So I will too."

"Shirts would also be good," added Quinn, feeling the sting of the sun on his naked back. If nothing else, he wouldn't feel as vulnerable if he was covered.

Tomas nodded, and disappeared.

Quinn could hear his own breathing, despite the noise of the battle still raging around them.

"Is it just me, or is the blood slowing?" he asked after a few moments.

"It is," said Ash, with a relieved half smile. "I think we did it, Quinn. There's still a long way to go – I've got to clean the wound for starters. But at least the bleeding is stopping."

Jubilant, Quinn looked around for someone to tell – and noticed with growing horror that the battle was over. Cleaver, Abel, Dilly and Ison were being manhandled to the rail and tied together. Cook and Jericho were still fighting bravely, but with four Deslonders moving towards them, it was only a matter of time before they joined the others. There was no sign of Kurt, Tomas or the cleric.

"Um, Ash," he said, turning back to her. "What do you need to do to get Zain ready to be moved?"

"What?" she said. "We can't move him!"

"We're not going to have a choice," he said, urgently. "What do you need?"

"I need to bandage him up," she said, voice rising with panic. "I need sheets or something to make bandages – I should have told Tomas!"

Quinn nodded. "I'll be back in a minute."

Ducking low, he crept to the stairs, eyes fixed on the *Libertas* crew, struggling with their captors. Quinn swallowed hard against the nausea swelling up in his throat. This was all his fault!

Blinking back tears, he slid down the stairs as quietly as he could, running into Tomas at the bottom. "They're all caught," Quinn whispered urgently. "All of them. Take the blanket to Ash while I get some sheets."

"We need to hide if we can," said Tomas, pulling a blue shirt over his head and thrusting a white one at Quinn. "There's no point in us all being taken captive."

"You're right," said Quinn, though he wondered how that would work on a boat the size of the *Libertas*. "I'll grab the sheets from Zain's cabin – it's closest. Can you take them up to Ash and then get back down here? I'll hide the maps and anything else I can think of."

Tomas nodded, following Quinn into the big cabin at the end of the passage. As he pushed the door open, Quinn thought he heard a scuttling sound, but the cabin was dark and he couldn't see anything unusual. *Must have been overhead*, he thought.

"Here," he said, pulling back Zain's plain woolen blanket, and pulling the sheet from the bed. Tomas took it and disappeared.

Scanning the cabin, Quinn noticed once again how neat and tidy it was. Nothing out of place. Zain had hidden all his papers, along with the loganstones, in the various hidey-holes in the cabin walls – the location of which were known only to him. The sack of starstone "rocks," on the other hand, was tucked neatly in a corner, hiding in plain sight.

After Quinn had shown Zain the secret he'd uncovered at the heart of his rock, the captain had decided it was safest to leave all the others as "rocks" and treat them as though they had no value. If you didn't know what they were, you'd have no reason to look at them twice – and only a handful of people on the *Libertas* knew their true value.

Satisfied that all was as it should be, Quinn backed out of the room and closed the door, heading to his own cabin where he quickly shoved the map under a loose floorboard. The real map should be safe enough in its hiding place in the cleric's room, he decided, giving his own cabin one last look. As he did so, Quinn heard the snick of a door down the passage.

Very carefully, he opened his door a finger width, peering out just in time to see Kurt letting himself out of Zain's cabin.

"What are you doing?" shouted Quinn, stepping into the passage.

Kurt froze, and Quinn could see that his face was nearly as white as his hair, but he recovered quickly when he saw that it was only Quinn challenging him. "Nothing," he said sulkily. "None of your business."

"It is my business," said Quinn, striding down the passage to grab the Northern boy by the arm. "What did you just do?"

Kurt squinted up at Quinn. "Just checking that everything's safe," he muttered. "Same as you. Or *is* that what you were doing?"

The blood rushed to Quinn's ears. "*Of course* that's what I was doing," he choked.

"So you say," said Kurt, turning away. Fuming, Quinn tried to pull him back, but Kurt bucked and writhed like an eel. There was a thud at Quinn's feet, and he looked down to see a rock lying there.

"Empty your pockets!" Quinn shouted, bending to pick it up, even as he grasped Kurt's arm more firmly.

"Make me," said the Northern boy, jabbing at Quinn's head with his knee.

Before he could think, Quinn stood and punched Kurt hard in the soft place under his ribs.

"Oof," said Kurt, doubling over. "I can't wait to tell Zain that you hit me."

Quinn could hardly see straight for the anger that rose up in him at the thought that this horrible boy was using Zain against him while Zain was lying bleeding all over the deck above. He raised his fist again –

"Well, well, well," said a strange voice behind him in Deslondic. "Looky here. They're fighting each other – guess that saves us from doing it." The comment was greeted with loud guffawing.

Quinn turned slowly to see three of the men from the dragon boat standing at the bottom of the stairs, blocking the sunlight from above – and any hope of escape.

Chapter Nine

"Where's Tomas?" Ash whispered, lips barely moving.

They were crammed together in the stern of the *Libertas*, hands tied behind their backs, Zain sitting woozily beside them, leaning against the water barrel. The only person who looked less healthy than Zain was the cleric, who was blinking in the sunlight, propped between Jericho and Cleaver.

Quinn waited until the Deslonder who was strolling up and back, "guarding" them, had walked away, taking his sharp, pointed stick with him, before replying. "I don't know," he said. "Last time I saw him, he was on his way back to you with the blanket and sheet."

Both were now wrapped around Zain, suggesting that Tomas had gotten at least that far. Quinn hoped that Tomas was free and hiding somewhere, rather than lying in a pool of blood out of sight.

Having been herded into this small section and trussed together, the *Libertas* crew could only watch as the Deslonders took over their ship. A small number had remained on the dragon boat, which was even now jubilantly leading the *Libertas* into port.

Quinn's eyes widened as he took in the view ahead – the sand-colored buildings seemed to glow in the bright sunlight. Each was topped with a domed roof that had been tiled in different colors, creating a patchwork of blues and reds and yellows and oranges against the turquoise sky.

"It's beautiful," whispered Ash.

"It is Katinhara," Zain murmured, eyes half-closed, taking in his first view of his homeland in more than twenty years. "Busiest port in Deslond."

"The capital?" asked Ash.

"No, Fesna is farther inland," said Zain slowly, staring at the port, though Quinn suspected his thoughts were far away. "Seat of the emperor, and nearer my home village. There the colors are even brighter."

They waited, but he said no more. Quinn tried hard to imagine a younger version of his sober, sensible captain growing up in this hard, clear light, surrounded by these vivid colors. The contrast with Verdania and its soft grays, greens and browns could not be more marked. What a shock it must have been for Zain when he'd first arrived in Oakston . . .

"I just wish we were visiting under different circumstances," said Quinn.

This time Zain merely grunted, and Ash turned to him in concern. He was sweating profusely and his weathered face, under the scars, was pale.

"Not quite what I had in mind," he managed, before subsiding once again into silence.

The captive crew all looked at him and shook their heads, worrying Quinn even more than Zain's rasping voice. They were tied together with heavy ropes – much more so than Quinn and Ash, or even Kurt, whom the Deslonders had placed well away from Quinn; the only plus to the whole situation.

"What are we going to do, Quinn?" Ash breathed.

Quinn closed his eyes momentarily. He was hot, thirsty and that horrible pain had begun throbbing in his head. But if he didn't come up with something, they were all going to end up in a Deslondic prison – and from what Cleaver had muttered to him, that was nowhere *anyone* wanted to be.

So far the dragon boat crew had ignored all pleas for a parley from the crew. Quinn had overheard worrying conversations from their captors that included words like "traitors" and "spies for Verdania" and "war."

"The trouble is," Cleaver had said in low-voiced Deslondic to the other crew members, unaware that Quinn could understand, "we don't have a leg to stand on. The law of the sea says we're in the wrong – and we're flying a Verdanian flag."

Now, Quinn swallowed hard, willing his overwhelmed mind to come up with something – anything! And then he became aware of a tugging sensation at the ropes that bound his hands.

"Don't move," a voice hissed behind him.

Tomas!

Looking sideways without moving his head, Quinn could see his friend stretched out on his stomach, half of him obscured by the water barrel, the rest hiding behind Zain and Quinn himself.

"Now you do Ash," Tomas whispered, and Quinn realized that his hands were free. Quickly, he reached behind Ash, and began pulling at the knot, as Tomas scrambled back behind Zain. "Keep them tied loosely," Tomas instructed, "so that they don't suspect you're free."

Quinn looped the rope back around his own hands.

"If we can get free, we can work out how to rescue the others," Tomas was saying in a low voice.

"I can't leave Zain," Ash whispered urgently.

"Yes, you can," said Zain, and Quinn realized he was listening to everything around him, even though he looked asleep. "You must."

Ash bit her lip. "I'm worried," she said.

Zain managed a half smile. "So am I," he admitted, "but you're of more use to me outside a dungeon – and I don't want them discovering you're a girl."

Ash realized the sense in this and nodded.

After that, there was no more conversation and they all sat in tense silence as they felt the *Libertas* bump and shudder as she was inexpertly guided into dock.

"Our one chance for escape will be the transfer from ship to land." Tomas's voice came ghostlike from behind the barrel.

Quinn nodded slightly to indicate he'd heard, his mind working furiously to come up with a plan. "We need a diversion," he said under his breath to Ash.

"Do not worry about that," said Zain slowly. "Leave it to me."

Quinn glanced sideways at his captain, who didn't look capable of raising his eyelids, let alone causing a diversion. "Leave it to me, Quinn Freeman," Zain said, leaving Quinn to wonder if he could actually see with his eyes closed.

There was another creaking shudder, and then the dragon boat crew was throwing ropes down to the dock, shouting cheerfully at the men helping them to moor the *Libertas*. They tied the ship securely, with two thick ropes in the bow, side by side, and two in the stern to match.

Zain had lifted his head to watch. "Those ropes are your way out," he said.

Ash looked at Quinn in alarm, but he nodded.

"Cleaver," Zain was saying, and the first mate shifted his head slightly so that he could see his captain. "When I give the signal, the old Deslondic welcome."

Cleaver frowned. "Really?" he asked.

Zain nodded.

Cleaver sighed. "If you insist." He turned to whisper to Abel, beside him, and Quinn could see the message telegraphed along the line.

No more was said until the *Libertas* was secured and the gangplank was sliding over the side to meet the dock.

"Now!" Zain whispered urgently.

Suddenly, the *Libertas* crew were all struggling to their feet, dragging the thick ropes, the cleric and Kurt with them. Once they were all up, they began stamping and singing, shouting and hollering, and generally creating an almighty racket. Using the water barrel for support, Zain dragged himself up to join them, maneuvering himself into position behind the line of crewmen.

At first, the dragon boat crew stood, staring, mouths open, but then they rushed forward as one to quell the uprising.

Zain turned to Ash and Quinn, shouting "NOW," even as the *Libertas* crew threw themselves at their captives, using the rope to entangle and trip them, before falling into a writhing heap of arms and legs.

Quinn ran for the nearest rope and swung himself up and over the side of the *Libertas*, shinnying down the taut rope towards the dock. As his head disappeared over the side, he saw Zain suddenly fall forward into the line of crewmen in front of him, squashing the melee beneath him and adding to the confusion.

Quinn winced, knowing how much that move would have hurt Zain's injured shoulder.

"Go!" said Tomas, who had reached the rail. "Go now!"

With one last look at the teeming, rolling mass of arms and legs on the deck, Quinn went, sliding down the rope so fast that it burned him through his breeches. Ash, who had not stopped to watch the other crew members, was just touching lightly down on the dock, tucking herself in behind some crates that had been unloaded from the ship on the other side of the pier.

Quinn slithered to the bottom of the rope and went to join her, with Tomas squishing in beside them moments later. They stayed there, gasping for breath, watching the throng of people on the dock. Quinn noticed, to his relief, that the crowd was mixed, with faces from many places – it would be much easier to blend in to a group like that, even if their Verdanian attire did look different.

"What do we do now?" Tomas asked as, moments later, they watched the *Libertas* crew being herded down the gangplank. Zain and Cleric Greenfield brought up the rear, and Quinn noted that, even in as much pain as he was,

Zain was careful to support the elderly man on the narrow plank. Kurt was between Jericho and Cleaver and looked as though he'd swallowed a dozen lemons.

"We follow," said Quinn. "And then . . ."

"Then?" prompted Ash.

"We'll work it out," said Quinn, with more confidence than he felt. He was hoping that the holes in his memory weren't interfering with the working of the rest of his mind.

They watched anxiously as the crew was hustled to the end of the pier, then Quinn stood up. "Come on," he said, stepping out from behind the crates, with Ash and Tomas at his heels. "Try to look relaxed," he told Tomas, who was standing stiffly, peering about him.

"Oh, right," Tomas squeaked. "Relaxed."

Ash laughed. "Okay, if not relaxed, then perhaps less like you're expecting twenty Deslonders to jump on you at any moment."

Tomas took a deep breath, and his hunched shoulders dropped visibly.

"That's better," said Ash, sauntering nonchalantly down the pier, looking for all the world like she was killing time waiting for a ship to load.

Quinn grinned, and followed her lead. As they strolled in the sunshine, however, his eyes were darting this way and that, watching the *Libertas* crew disappearing up the dusty road and taking note of the ships in the port. There was a heavy sprinkling of dragon boats, which were clearly the transportation of choice in these parts. He noticed ships from Athelstan and even the Northern kingdoms bobbing in the next dock, and took in the lines of a particularly beautiful Frenz ship.

And then his heart sank. "Look," he said, nudging Ash. "The *Wandering Spirit* is here."

She stopped to stare, and he nudged her to keep moving before they attracted attention. "Maybe they'll help us?" she said doubtfully.

Quinn thought of Ira pushing him down into a deep pit in Barbarin. "I think we should stay well out of their way," he said.

Tomas tugged the back of his shirt. "I think we've got bigger problems than them," he said, pointing out into the bay, where the ships docked for longer-term visits. "That's the Golden Serpent's ship."

Quinn froze. Last time he'd seen the pirate ship it had been drifting off in the middle of the endless ocean. He turned and scanned the rest of the port with urgent eyes.

"Do you see the *Black Hawk?*" he asked.

"No," said Ash.

"Which is not to say the Gelynions aren't here," said Tomas, still staring at the pirate ship. "The *Black Hawk* was damaged by fire at sea, remember? We do not know who is aboard the Golden Serpent's ship, but chances are Juan Forden is here."

Quinn swallowed hard. If he never saw Juan Forden and Morpeth again it would be too soon. "How did they get here before us?" he wondered aloud.

"You heard Egunon," said Tomas. "The Golden Serpent knows these waters well. He would have sailed straight here to regroup."

Quinn shuddered. "All the more reason to get Zain and the others and get out of here," he said. "Let's go!"

This time, there was no strolling as they turned and ran after the disappearing *Libertas* crew.

Chapter Ten

Quinn was hot, thirsty and frustrated, but he kept telling himself that if he felt bad, then Zain and the others felt worse. Shifting uncomfortably, he earned himself a sharp look from Ash and a rueful smile from Tomas. They were hiding in the shadow of a domed building that seemed to be constructed from blocks of sand, staring across the dusty road at another, smaller, domed building with barred windows. Three men sat near the doorway, apparently playing a game, judging by the occasional shouts, laughter and curses. They were huddled together in the scant shade provided by a thin, straggly tree. Quinn had noticed a decided lack of vegetation in this town, and wondered if it was typical of Deslond.

"How long have we been here?" asked Tomas for the fourth time.

"About half a tick since you last asked," said Ash wearily.

"Have you thought of a plan yet?" Tomas asked Quinn.

"No," sighed Quinn, turning his thoughts away from the local flora.

"Can we at least go and find some water while you think?" asked Tomas.

"You'll only get lost," said Ash.

"Well, Quinn can go then," said Tomas. "He should remember the way back."

Quinn gulped. *Should* was the operative word there. But he didn't want his friends to know about his head, which even now was hurting him.

"Sure," he said. "I think I remember seeing a well with a dipper a bit farther back. I'll come up with a plan on the way."

Ash gave him another sharp look at his use of the word "think," but he managed a smile and darted off down the alley. As he ran, he realized that all the alleys looked the same – dusty underfoot and surrounded by high walls of those sand bricks. In Markham, the houses were all small white cottages, but at least people used milk paint to change the color of their doors, so you could tell strangers "third street on the right, blue door." Here, there were no such markers.

Reaching a four-way intersection he paused, looking left, then right. This way. No . . . that way. Cursing under his breath, he turned right, slowing his pace. Was it here?

The alley was very quiet, with only the tiniest breeze to stir the dirt under his feet.

It was too quiet, he decided. When they'd followed Zain and the others to the jail, the alleys had been wider, more populated.

He stopped.

"So," said a voice behind him, "you managed to escape the pit."

Whirling around, Quinn found himself facing Ira, who was standing, hands on hips, feet apart, blocking Quinn's exit from the alley. "No thanks to you," he replied bitterly.

Ira's laugh was harsh and forced. "No," he agreed. "No thanks to me. But here you are. Like a bad centime, always turning up. I would have thought a farm boy would have been left behind by now."

Quinn's anger rose in him, nearly blinding him with its force. Without even thinking, he launched himself at Ira, kicking out his right leg and sweeping the boy's feet from under him. Both boys crashed to the ground, and Quinn had one sweet moment of satisfaction before he realized that Ira was on top of him – and he was bigger and stronger!

He was glad of Zain's intensive training because his body remembered what to do, even as his mind froze. Hands in front of his face, he instinctively rolled out from under Ira and was on his feet before Ira knew what was happening.

"That was for the pit," he said, as Ira staggered to his feet with a growl. "This one is for everything else." With that, he put all the darkness and frustration he'd felt while stuck in the hold of the *Black Hawk* into one swinging punch, collecting Ira on the side of the jaw, and welcoming the agonizing pain that reverberated through his own hand and up his arm.

Ira swayed wildly, but did not fall as Quinn had hoped.

"Is that it?" the blond boy smirked, though Quinn noticed a quaver in his voice. "Is that all you've got?"

Quinn paused. Was that it?

The half-moment hesitation was all Ira needed and, with a yell, he was on Quinn, tackling him to the dusty path. Quinn fell backward, trying desperately to break his fall, but his head hit the path with a crack and the world went blurry. Still Ira pummeled him, rolling him over and over while Quinn tried desperately to fight the whirling sensation behind his eyebrows and the nausea surging through him.

Eyes full of dirt, Quinn clutched at Ira's hair, pulling for all he was worth, trying to get a moment to breathe, to think, to stop the bright lights flashing with every movement. Ira cursed, flinging his head back, and Quinn was left holding a hunk of blond hair.

"You peasant!" Ira screamed, rubbing his head hard with one hand, before throwing himself forward to pin both Quinn's shoulders, holding his upper body immobile.

Strangely, it was just what Quinn needed to steady himself and he stilled, going limp under Ira's grip, grappling with the strange sensation of seeing his whole life flickering before him as picture after picture flooded his mind.

For a moment, he wondered what was happening to him – and then he gasped. His memory was coming back! The blow to the head had somehow jogged free whatever blockage he'd been experiencing and those pictures that had been with him always, that he'd relied upon for so much of this journey, were all falling back into place.

Lying in the dirt, with a bruise already forming on his stomach from Ira's beating, Quinn began to laugh with relief.

"What are you laughing at, you runt?" An infuriated Ira redoubled his efforts, using his knees to punish Quinn, even as he kept him pinned to the ground. Quinn realized that Ira had superior size and strength, but that he was flailing about and most of his blows weren't very effective.

Quinn grinned up at him. With the return of his memory, he felt confidence flooding through him – and he'd had enough of Ira. "You," he said simply. "I'm laughing at you."

With that, he drew his knee up hard and fast into Ira's stomach. As Ira gasped, winded, Quinn grabbed him by the top of his breeches and pulled hard, while thrusting his own legs up, using them to push Ira up and forward, over Quinn's head and face-first into the dirt behind him, where Ira lay, stunned and wheezing. Quinn jumped to his feet, and turned lightly, ready to defend himself. But Ira merely scrabbled about in the dirt, whimpering, his face covered in dust, blood now dripping from the spot where Quinn had pulled his hair.

Quinn drew back his boot, wanting to hurt Ira – *really* hurt him. But, suddenly, he could hear his father's voice in his ear. "You don't kick a boy when he's down," his da was saying, "unless you want to kill him, which is a whole different story." With six sons, Beyard Freeman had broken up more than his fair share of wrestling matches, and he'd gone out of his way to instill the rules of fair play very early – for which Quinn, as the youngest and smallest, had always been grateful.

As Ira whimpered again, struggling to catch his breath, Quinn quietly lowered his boot to the ground before stepping over to nudge the boy with his toe.

"Do not come near me again," he said to Ira. "Do not speak to me again. Do not look at me again."

"Pah," Ira panted, spitting out dirt. "You got lucky."

Quinn laughed, hard and low, and put his boot on Ira's chest. "Maybe," he said. "But we'll call it even. I got a face full of dirt in Barbarin, you got a face full of dirt here. Besides, I've got more important things to do."

With that, he turned and darted back up the alley, suddenly sure of his directions. His head ached a little from the impact of the blow, and he was covered in dirt, but Quinn hadn't felt happier in weeks.

It was time to rescue Zain and the others, get out of here and win the race around the world.

Chapter Eleven

Quinn frowned, squinting up once again at the facade of the tiny shop. Yes, this was the place. It looked much like every other building around it, but the crescent shape cut into the bricks halfway up had jogged his memory as soon as he'd seen it.

He looked around the corner once more, and shook his head. This should be the small square in which the well was located, but how would he know? It was currently crowded with people, all encircling a speaker, whose voice he could hear rising and falling over the muttering of the crowd, which was blocking his view.

There was nothing for it – he was going to have to squeeze in there to see if this was, in fact, the right place.

Keeping close to the wall, he crept down the alley, finding his way blocked by people at the opening to the square. The speaker's voice was louder . . . and strangely familiar.

Quinn began pushing his way through the bodies around him – very tall, heavy bodies.

"Oops, sorry, excuse me," Quinn muttered, automatically speaking Deslondic and wondering what Deslonders ate to get so large. Even the women were much taller than him, which surprised him. He was slight, but he'd been catching up to his mam when he'd left Verdania.

He continued to squeeze through the sweaty crush, envying the Deslonders their cool clothing. Everyone here wore the same thing – breezy, flowing pants and a thin, long-sleeved tunic, always in white. Quinn wondered why there were no colors, given how dazzling all that white was in the harsh sunlight and the hues of the tiled roofs around him, but reasoned it must have something to do with keeping cool.

He was now within two rows of the speaker, standing between two Zain-sized men, still unable to see but able to hear what was being said.

"He will soon arrive," the deep voice intoned. "The traitor is on his way and it is essential that we do everything we can to stop him. To jail him. To hang him like the dog he is."

The men on either side of Quinn erupted into cheers, along with the rest of the crowd.

"He sold us out to the Verdanians!" the voice continued, passionate and hard. And suddenly Quinn knew who that voice belonged to. Dropping to his knees, he crawled cautiously through the rows of legs in front of him until he was able to see the speaker clearly.

And there, even larger than Quinn remembered, was Morpeth, dressed in the same flowing white pants and tunic as the other Deslonders, with Juan Forden at his side. Quinn scanned the crowd but could see no sign of the Golden Serpent.

"He shall go down in the history books as Zain the Destroyer!" Morpeth was shrieking. "He killed every member of his own village to impress the Verdanians and then convinced our king to sign a treaty that made a mockery of Deslondic pride!"

Quinn was stunned. What was he talking about?

"And then . . ." said Morpeth, voice lowered. "And then he went to Verdania to share all the secrets of Deslondic warfare with our greatest enemy."

Nooooo! Quinn wanted to shout. It wasn't like that. It couldn't have been.

Quinn scuttled back between the crowds of legs, searching for a spot at the back where he could still hear Morpeth but would have less chance of being spotted.

"We must be watchful!" Morpeth was shouting. "Watch the port! Watch the docks! At first sign of him, Zain must be arrested. He must be made to pay the price for treason and treachery!"

They didn't know they had Zain. Quinn tried to muster his thoughts, realizing he was gasping for breath. He had to get back to that prison and get Zain out before Morpeth and the rest of this angry mob realized he was already in Katinhara! Mind reeling and full of questions, Quinn darted back through the twisting, winding alleys, desperate to get to the jail. As he ran, his thoughts came faster and faster. Was what Morpeth had said about Zain true? Quinn remembered Zain's scary Hayreddin persona and the awful determination on his face as he'd held Egunon over that cliff.

Struck with horror by his own thoughts, Quinn stopped dead. What was he thinking? This was Zain. Dignified, loyal, strong, patient Zain. There was no way that Morpeth's words were true – but somewhere in them lay the heart of the ill feeling between the two Deslonders.

Shaking his head to clear his thoughts, he set off again, running headlong around a corner – and straight into a body running the other way, throwing Quinn off balance and sending him down into the dirt for the umpteenth time that day.

"Oof! Watch where you're going!"

Wiping dirt from his eyes, Quinn laughed out loud at the sound of that voice. "Ajax!" he shouted.

His red-haired friend, busy picking himself up from the sandy alley, started. "Quinn!" Ajax stepped forward to help Quinn to his feet, and Quinn marveled yet again at the sheer size of his friend. He was no Zain, but, at fourteen,

Ajax was nearly as big as Simon, Quinn's nineteen-year-old brother.

"Where are you going in such a hurry?" asked Quinn.

"Bah," said Ajax. "I was running away from a bunch of old ladies down in that alley." He gestured wildly behind him.

Quinn laughed again. "Old ladies?"

"I don't think they've ever seen red hair before," said Ajax with a grimace. "Everywhere I go, someone wants to stroke my head. It's driving me crazy."

It was such a relief to laugh that Quinn lost control, dissolving into a fit of giggles that would have made Merry, Simon's lady love, proud.

"Oh stop!" said Ajax, playfully cuffing him around the head. "You're obviously in a good mood. No Gelynions chasing you today?"

Quinn sobered instantly. "*Leif's boots!*" he said. The joy of seeing Ajax had driven all other thoughts from his mind, but now they came flooding back. "I have so much to tell you – but now is not the time. Come with me!"

Ajax nodded, falling in beside Quinn as he took off towards the jail. "Where are we going?"

"To rescue Zain," Quinn said grimly.

Ajax grunted. "Zain?"

"It's a long story, but we need to get to him before Morpeth finds out he's here," gasped Quinn, beginning to feel a stitch in his side from all the running around in the heat.

Ajax stopped. "Morpeth? Isn't he the one who . . . how did you get away from them? Last time I saw you, you were down a pit and I . . . Oh, Quinn, I'm sorry about leaving you there – and so ashamed of Odilon."

Quinn touched his friend's arm briefly. "You had no choice," he said, drawing in deep breaths while they were stopped. "As for Odilon . . . where is he anyway?"

"At the docks," said Ajax. "Preparing to sail. We've been here a day already. He's all stocked up and preparing to get back to Verdania. Now that he's arrived somewhere familiar, he's cocky. Reckons he's got the race sewn up – particularly as there was no sign of Dolan or the *Libertas*."

"Dolan is here," said Quinn, remembering with quiet satisfaction his last sighting of Ira.

"Then Odilon will want to go sooner rather than later," fretted Ajax. "He's been making me use that map of yours, Quinn. I just . . ." The big redhead's fists clenched in frustration. "It's not right," he finished.

"Don't worry about that," said Quinn, thinking of his own "real" map. "Just do what you need to do to get through this. I don't want him to have any reason to leave you behind."

"He could," said Ajax, gloomily. "It's not like he hasn't done it before, and the basic maps between here and Verdania will allow him to finish the race."

"Don't think about it," said Quinn. "Come with me now, and help with Zain, then head back to the *Fair Maiden*. I want to get this done as quickly as possible, and I don't want Odilon to find out Zain is in prison. He and Morpeth are too friendly. Will you help me?"

"I will." Ajax nodded. "It's the least I can do after Zain saved me."

"Let's get to it then," said Quinn, already moving and thinking hard. It was one thing to say they were going to rescue Zain – and quite another thing to do it.

Chapter Twelve

"I can't see how we're going to do this." Ajax voiced what Quinn was thinking.

They were tucked into the shadow of the building opposite the jail, next to Tomas and Ash, who had both been thrilled to see them – and extremely disappointed that Quinn had not brought water.

"They just sit there, playing that game," said Tomas. "They never leave, not even to go for a walk."

"We have to get past them to get the others out," said Quinn, slapping his hand on the wall in frustration, aware of time ticking away. He'd told the others that he'd spotted Morpeth – but hadn't shared his words with them. He didn't want to even say them out loud. If he kept them to himself, it made them seem less real.

"*No-o-t* necessarily," said Ash, watching as the guards threw coins into the circle to begin yet another round of the game.

All three boys looked at her in surprise.

"How's your Deslondic these days, Quinn?" she asked.

"Okay," he said slowly. He thought a moment, relief flooding through him as all his memories of the Deslondic language filled his mind. "Actually, more than okay," he said.

"Good," she said. "Now, what have you got to bet with?"

"Bet?" he asked, confused. Of all the questions he could imagine her asking, that one was not on the list.

"Bet," she said, impatiently. "Turn out your pockets."

Everyone emptied their pockets. Tomas had *cacao* dust. Ajax and Ash had nothing. Quinn had the starstone rock he'd taken from Kurt.

"Is that what I think it is?" asked Ash, pointing at it.

"Yes," he replied.

"Break it," she said, handing over her knife. "Make it shine."

Picking up a large rock from the alley, he did as she asked, ignoring Ajax's hiss of breath as the "rock" sheared off and the inner, twinkling center was revealed.

"Right," said Ash, pointing to the door of the jail where the game was now ending in a barrage of shouts and insults. "Go over there and win Zain."

Quinn looked at her, eyebrows raised.

"Bet your starstone and win the game," continued Ash. "You can do that, can't you?" She looked at him closely, and he knew that she'd suspected more about his faulty memory than he'd realized.

"Yes," he told her quietly. "I can do that."

"You get through that door and we'll follow you in and help," said Ash, her voice full of determination.

"*Ri-i-ght*," said Ajax. "So you're just going to wander over there and join the game?" He looked half-worried, half-skeptical.

"Yes," said Ash, "he is."

At that, there was nothing for it but that Quinn should wander across the road towards the jail. He pushed his hands deep into his pockets, trying to look nonchalant, but clutching the starstone tightly. As he got closer, he saw the guard leaning against the door, facing the road, nudge the others. They all stopped their game to watch him approach.

"Er, hello," he stammered as he reached them. They stared at him.

"I was wondering if I could join in," Quinn rushed on, noticing how the men jumped at his use of their language. They were a rough-looking bunch, each sporting scars on their faces.

"You are not from here," said the Door Man, spitting a large, viscous chunk into the dirt at Quinn's feet.

Quinn watched it wobble there, feeling slightly ill. "No," he said, "but I can buy in." He'd heard Jericho use that expression when playing the game with Ison and Dilly, usually throwing an uneaten hard biscuit or a centime into the center. The stakes today would be much higher.

The men laughed. "Is that so?" said Door Man. "And what would a *piccoli* like you have to offer?" He chortled, and his long, curling black hair swung around his face.

Quinn swallowed. *Piccoli* meant "little baby." But then he managed a smile. He'd been called worse – the Gelynions had christened him "Monstruo Mouse," basically calling him a little freak. Baby was a step up.

"I have this," he said, holding the starstone above them so that it glittered and shone in the sunlight.

Door Man sat up straight. "Is that so?" he said, dark eyes shining with greed. "Well, now, I think we can find room for you here."

The others moved around slightly to create a small space for Quinn. "I am Yanda," said Door Man. "This is Vartan." He indicated the skinny man to his right. "And Artus." Artus nodded, his bald head gleaming in the sun. "Right," Yanda continued. "Let's play."

"Not so fast," Quinn said, his mouth suddenly dry. "If I'm putting this up, you will also need to offer a worthy prize." He tried to sound more confident than he felt – really, there was no reason for these men not to simply jump on him and take the stone.

The men looked at each other, and muttered together briefly, just low enough so Quinn could not hear.

"We will put these up," said Yanda. He and the others threw their battered knives into the circle.

Quinn liked the idea that at least he now knew where their knives were – but he wasn't sure if they'd stay on the ground with his next words. "Not enough," he said, looking down.

"Why you . . ." Vartan stood – he was so tall and skinny that Quinn wondered if he was related to Abel. He looked down at the man's feet, which were average in size. Not Abel then, whose feet were huge.

"Wait!" Yanda grabbed his friend's arm, pulling him back down, where he sat on the ground with a thump and a very unhappy expression. "You obviously have something in mind," he continued. "And given that you look Verdanian to me, I'm thinking it has something to do with that old man in there."

Quinn was startled. It hadn't occurred to him that the only members of the captured *Libertas* crew who looked Verdanian were Cleric Greenfield and, perhaps, Kurt. He'd been so centered on Zain, who, of course, looked Deslondic, that he'd completely forgotten about the kindly old cleric. Kurt he tried never to consider.

He thought quickly, deciding that it was much less suspicious for him to try to win the cleric's freedom. Once the door was opened, they could . . . well, Quinn wasn't sure what exactly they'd do yet, but getting the cleric out was a start. All he knew was that he needed to get going

– how long could it possibly take before Morpeth and Forden heard about the strange crew being held captive? Or someone spotted the *Libertas* down at the docks?

"Yes," Quinn said now, nodding. "That's right. The old man. I want him. If I win, I get to take him. If you win, you get this shiny rock."

Yanda's eyes glinted again, and he nodded. Quinn knew that he was very aware of the value of the starstone.

"We begin – first player to win three rounds takes all," Yanda announced, and Quinn bent down to place his rock in the circle as the first tiles were drawn. Sweat gathered on his brow as he watched Vartan throw out the first tile, hoping that these Deslonders played the game in the same way as the *Libertas* crew.

As play proceeded, all he could hear was the click-click of the tiles as the men around him shuffled them in their hands, then dropped them deliberately onto the pile. Quinn sat perfectly still, aware of a dog barking somewhere in the neighborhood, and the call of seabirds as they wheeled around the crowded dock a short distance away. He could almost feel the force of Ash's stare on the back of his neck, knowing that she and Tomas and Ajax were watching intently from across the road. He forced himself to concentrate, mentally counting, keeping track in his mind of what was out in the circle to give him a better idea of what each man held. Click, click, click. Six triangles, one triangle, three squares.

Quinn played carefully, not wanting to give away the fact that he knew what he was doing, and watched each man closely. Jericho had told him that every player had a "tell" – something they did if they were excited about their next move. The trick was to learn what that thing was so that you could play your own tiles accordingly.

Yanda tugged his ear, then threw out a winning tile. *One.*

Vartan jiggled his knee before he made his next move. *Two.*

The dog's barking became more persistent and was joined by the howl of another dog closer by. Quinn stirred – something was happening to rouse the animals. He refocused on the game, realizing that they were getting down to the last three rounds. He needed to be on his guard now.

Artus sighed, deep and low, telling Quinn everything he needed to know about the hand the man held. He looked down at his own tiles – he needed to play the next three rounds right if he was to win.

Flicking back through his memory, he realized that most of the valuable tiles had been played. He was happy that he had fallen into the position of being the last player to put his tile down in this round.

Yanda tugged his ear, even as Vartan's knee began jiggling. Both men were getting ready to play what they thought were their winning tiles. Quinn stared at his hand, calculating the possibilities of what the other players held, and waited.

Sure enough, Vartan tossed down six triangles with a "Ha!" Yanda smiled smugly, before placing six squares deliberately on top, and Vartan's face fell. Artus sighed again before throwing four circles listlessly onto the pile. He knew he was beaten.

Quinn pretended to consider his tiles, before putting down three squares, and mimicking Artus's defeated expression, as though pushing the round over the magic forty-two wasn't part of his plan. Yanda gathered all the tiles together, chortling.

"Just two more rounds, *piccoli*," he said. "I think that you are beaten."

Quinn tried to look glum. The truth was, however, that he knew what the others held and knew that his four circles and five squares were enough to beat them. He just had to play them in the right order. And it was his turn to play first this round.

Taking a deep breath, he put down the four circles, praying to all the gods in all the world that he'd calculated right. A sharp intake of breath to his left suggested that Vartan was out of the game, and sure enough, he dropped three circles next to Quinn's tile. Artus simply sighed again, and Quinn dismissed him from contention. Yanda stared at Quinn's tile, deliberating between two in his hand, but his fingers stayed away from his ear, suggesting that he did not think he could win this round. Quinn held his breath, hoping that he had not miscalculated.

Yanda put down two squares. Quinn knew this had to be the lower-valued tile in his hand, but what else did Yanda have? Quinn thought hard, recalling a clear picture of the six-square tile – the highest-valued tile – being pulled out in the first round.

Yanda could not beat him.

Quinn gathered in the tiles and tried to look worried about the next and final round.

"So *piccoli*, we have won two each; Vartan has one, Artus has none," said Yanda. "The next round decides your old man's future."

The whole world seemed to pause as Vartan placed his tile down.

"You go next," said Yanda to Artus.

Quinn frowned. "That's not the order of the game."

"It is if I say so," said Yanda, and Quinn suddenly became aware again of how big the man was.

Artus shook his head. "We play fair," he said.

"Yeah," said Vartan. "You don't make the rules."

"Play. Next." Yanda's order was terse, and Artus sighed, shaking his head, but he put his tile down.

Yanda didn't even bother to look at it.

"Now you," he said to Quinn.

But Quinn shook his head, checking the circle to see that the three knives were still there, out in the open.

He thought he heard scuffling sounds behind him, but couldn't risk turning to look.

"No," he said. "You."

Yanda laughed, throwing back his head to reveal yellowing teeth.

"*Piccoli* has spine, I'll give him that."

He threw down his tile. Six squares.

"That's impossible," Quinn spluttered without thinking.

"What?" roared Yanda. "You accuse me of cheating?!"

All three men were on their feet.

"No!" said Quinn. "Yes!" His mind was in turmoil. How could he prove that Yanda had cheated? Who would believe that he remembered every move in the game? The man had obviously swapped the six-square piece for another as he'd dragged in the chips.

Vartan and Artus were shouting "Liar!" at the same time, but it took a moment for Quinn to understand that it wasn't he who was the object of their ire. Rather, it was Yanda!

"You cheat again!" screamed Vartan, and Quinn realized that this was an argument the men had had before.

"You would take the word of a boy, a stranger, over me?" hissed Yanda.

"He is only saying what we have been saying all morning," seethed Artus, shaking his fist. "Why should you win the starstone, not us?"

Yanda reached down to pull the starstone from the circle, holding it tightly in one hand.

"It's mine!" he shrieked, and the other two fell on him, pummeling and biting as they all rolled over in the dirt. Quinn was glad they'd forgotten their knives on the ground beside him – then again, if they all killed each other, it would make his job much easier.

"Don't just stand there, Quinn," said a voice to his right. "Try the door."

He looked over to see Ash, Ajax and Tomas all pressed against the side wall of the prison, trying to look inconspicuous. The scuttling sound he'd heard must have been them making their way over the road while the guards were distracted.

With one eye on the guards, still hissing and biting on the ground, Quinn ran quickly to the door and gave it a hard shove. It didn't budge.

Biting his lip, he turned back to the guards. "Stop!" he shouted in desperation. "You can have the starstone. Break it. Share it. I just want the old man."

"It's mine!" shouted Yanda. "I won it fair and square."

Quinn thought quickly. "Okay," he said. "If I tell the others you won it, will you let me have the key?"

If he could just get into the jail, he knew the *Libertas* crew would have no trouble taking care of these guards. Just to be sure, however, he bent down, picked up the three knives at his feet, and threw them gently in the direction of Ash, Ajax and Tomas.

"Say it!" demanded Yanda.

Quinn sighed. "Yanda won fair and square," he said, through clenched teeth.

The scuffling on the ground stilled briefly, and then a ring of keys slid across the dirt to land at his feet. Quinn didn't wait to see what happened next – he picked up the heavy ring and, grabbing the largest key and praying, turned and opened the door.

"Come on," he said to the others, who were staring at the grappling Deslonders in fascination. "They'll sort this argument out any minute, and then where will we be?"

"Hopefully on board the *Libertas*," said Ash, as she and the others followed Quinn inside.

"Lock the door behind us," said Ash.

"Why would I do that?" Quinn asked. "We need a quick getaway."

"To buy us some time," she said. "If those guards change their minds about letting us out of here, I want to be in charge of the door."

Quinn nodded, moving back to lock it behind them.

"How do we know where they are?" asked Ajax.

The small entryway in which Quinn and his friends were standing opened into a large circular space. Identical sturdy wooden doors lined the walls. There was no way to tell what was behind them.

"We don't," said Quinn. "We just open them all."

Unfortunately, this was easier said than done – none of the keys was marked, and they seemed to be in no particular order.

Quinn had to try every key in every door before finding the one that worked. His job was not made any easier by the fact that the prisoners began shouting and yelling and banging on the doors as soon as they heard the keys in the locks.

"*Leif's boots!* It's noisy in here," he cursed.

"That noise is not just coming from in here," said Tomas. "It's out there as well!"

Quinn froze, listening hard. Sure enough, the shrieking and yelling inside was augmented by the horrible babble of a mob of voices from outside the walls.

"What's going on?" whispered Ash, lips white with fear.

Quinn squeezed her shoulder, knowing that the sounds of the angry crowd were making her relive those horrible moments when she and her mother had been forced to leave Markham. "They're after Zain," he said, quickly filling them in on the scene in the square. "Morpeth was telling them terrible stories." He was not about to share the details of those stories right here.

"Morpeth?" said Ash.

"And Forden," confirmed Quinn. "I didn't want to scare you."

"Oh no," she said sarcastically. "Much better to find out like this."

"Come on," Ajax interrupted. "Get the others out, Quinn. We're going to need all the help we can get if we're to escape from here."

"I'll look for another way out," said Tomas. "There's always another way out."

Even in a jail? Quinn wanted to ask. He wasn't about to quell anybody's enthusiasm – but the truth was, he had a very bad feeling about their chances of making it out of this prison alive.

Chapter Thirteen

Breathing hard, Quinn approached the final door in the jail, the last key between his thumb and forefinger. Cleaver, Abel, Ison, Dilly, Jericho, the cleric and even Kurt had been relieved to see them when they opened the doors. Quinn had been surprised to come across three complete strangers, all Deslondic men, in one cell, and a man who reminded him of Egunon in another. All four were grateful to be let out, but horrified to be caught up in what could only be described as a siege.

Quinn assumed that Zain was behind this door . . . The door opened easily but, to Quinn's surprise, there was no room beyond it – just a dark, narrow hallway. He crept along and followed its curve.

Right at the end, he came to another small, strong door. Could this be the back door? Quinn pushed against the door, which didn't budge.

Quinn frowned, jingling the keys on his key ring. He

was sure he'd used them all, and didn't remember seeing one that might fit the tiny, round keyhole.

"Ajax!" he shouted. "Help me with this!"

Ajax ran down the hall from the central room.

"We've moved to the front cell so we can watch the crowd," he reported as he reached Quinn. "So far, they're just listening to Juan Forden's friend shouting, but I don't know how long that will last."

"Any sign of those three guards?" he asked.

Ajax shook his head. "Is this the back door?" he asked, looking over Quinn's shoulder in the dim light

"I don't know," said Quinn slowly. "Part of me hopes not, because if it is then Zain isn't in this building."

"Hmm," said Ajax. "Well, the part of me that wants to escape can't help but hope that it is."

"Whichever it is, there's no key!" Quinn said, jingling the key ring in frustration. "Can you do the hinges?"

Ajax had showed him a very nifty trick for opening a door from the "wrong" side by removing the hinges – and it had helped save all their lives in Kurt's frozen village.

Ajax frowned. "There are no hinges," he said, pointing to the door. "They're on the inside."

Quinn gulped. So much for that plan.

But Ajax was examining the lock. "It's a strange one," he said. "I think we could pick it if we had something hard and pointed. But it would need to fit in the hole."

Quinn threw his hands up. "Because, clearly, we have all manner of tools right here."

Ajax looked at him, injured. "I'm just saying, Quinn – do you want to get the door open, or do you want to be sarcastic?"

Quinn sighed. "Sorry," he muttered. "Wait here."

He ran back down the hall, to where everyone else was sitting dejectedly staring out the window at the growing crowd. "Empty your pockets," he found himself saying for the second time that day, repeating the order in Deslondic, much to the surprise of the crew.

A motley collection of coins, fluff, and rocks was paraded. Quinn noticed that Kurt had managed to hide whatever starstones were still in his possession. There was nothing that would help open the door.

"What do you need?" asked Ash.

"Something long, hard and pointed," he said.

"Like that?" she asked, pointing at his chest.

Quinn's hand crept up to the animal tooth hanging on a piece of leather around his neck. He was so used to wearing it that he didn't even remember it was there.

"Yes!" he shouted, dragging her to him for a hug, much to the amusement of the big Deslondic strangers, who no doubt assumed she was a boy. But Quinn had more important things to think about, and he was soon back at the door with Ajax.

"Try this," he said, pulling the leather thong over his head.

Ajax slid the pointed end of the tooth into the hole, and jiggled it up and down. They heard a faint click and the door opened a finger width.

Quinn was just about to push it open when Tomas huffed up to them. "I found a grille in one of the cells," he said, pointing to their left. "I think we'll be able to pull it out and escape that way."

"Go back and get the others," Quinn said. "I'll find Zain."

"Even if you do, he won't be able to climb out," said Tomas, panicked. "You saw him on the ship!"

Quinn thought fast. "We're going to need those Deslondic men," he said. "We'll have to hope they're grateful enough to help us out."

Ajax stared. "What are you thinking?"

"Go and get the biggest one and then come back and I'll explain," said Quinn, pushing the door open into a small, windowless room.

"It is good to see you, Quinn Freeman." Zain's breath was labored, and Quinn could only just make him out, lying on the floor against the wall.

"And you," Quinn said, quietly, trying not to let his worry sound through in his voice. "And looking so well."

Zain managed a laugh.

Ajax popped his head around the corner. "I've brought the man as you asked."

Quinn looked up to see the hulking Deslonder standing in the doorway, peering into the dark room, curiosity etched on every feature.

"Yes," said Quinn, nodding. "He'll do."

"Do for what?" asked Zain, and Quinn could hear a worrying breathiness in his voice.

"Do for you," said Quinn.

He went across to the man, speaking in low-voiced Deslondic.

"I don't know what you did to get in here," Quinn said, "but we can help you get out. Interested?"

The big man nodded, eyes narrowed.

"If you change clothes with him, you can go now."

The big man laughed. "Go where?" he said. "I will not get far out the front door."

"Out," said Quinn shortly. "I'll show you once you're dressed."

The man considered. "I have nothing to lose," he declared, beginning to strip off his white tunic.

"Can you get undressed?" Quinn asked Zain.

Zain nodded. "You will need to help with the shirt," he said. "But I can manage the rest . . . after you tell me what you have in mind."

"There is no time for that," Quinn said, striding back to Zain and beginning to ease the shirt over his injured shoulder. Zain winced, breath escaping with a hiss. Quinn was sorry to see him in pain but glad his attention was diverted. His plan was a hazy, half-formed thing and having to explain it right now was the last thing he wanted to do.

～

"I hope this works."

Quinn couldn't help but agree with Tomas. Ajax and Cleaver were busy trying to shove the hulking Deslondic prisoner through an air vent meant for a much smaller man.

"*Auugh*," said Cleaver, giving one last hard shove and the man finally disappeared through the grille with a strangely high-pitched yelp. Moments later they heard him crash to the ground outside. His two friends pushed forward and soon they were gone as well.

"So, you think the mob will chase them?" asked Cleaver, brushing his hands together. He was now wearing the Deslondic white robes, as was Jericho.

"I'm hoping they'll see three Deslonders dressed in Verdanian breeches, one covered in blood, and put two and two together," admitted Quinn.

"Pretty chancy," said Ajax.

Quinn could only nod, but his plan was based on the idea that people see what they want to see. He and Ash had used this theory to blend in places – now he was trying the idea in reverse.

"Go to the front cell and keep an eye on things," Quinn said. "I'm going to see how Zain's faring."

"Between him and Cleric Greenfield, we have some baggage to get back to the *Libertas*," said Cleaver, gloomily. "And an angry mob and some Gelynions between us and safety."

"If my plan works, we'll have lost the angry mob and the Gelynions," said Quinn. "But, yes, I am worried about the cleric as well."

The old man had been pale and confused when Quinn had released him from his cell. Ash had him lying on one of the hard, narrow beds, but he was not going to be easy to move.

"Ajax," Quinn said now, calling his friend back. "If that mob moves, you take care of the cleric and then go straight to the *Fair Maiden*. There's no reason for you to be tied up in all this."

"Ha!" said Ajax. "No reason at all but for the fact that I'd still be marooned in that tribal village if it wasn't for Zain."

"Well, if you get the cleric back to the *Libertas*, you'll have more than repaid your debt."

"What are you going to do?"

"Look after Zain," said Quinn.

"You can't carry him," said Ajax.

"Face it, nobody can carry him – I just need to get him moving and point him in the right direction."

"I hope you're right," said Ajax, "because otherwise you'll have to roll him all the way down to the docks."

A sudden shout went up from outside and Quinn looked at Ajax. "Go!" he said. "Now's the time."

Cleaver appeared in the doorway. "You were right, Quinn!" he yelled, eyes bright with excitement. "They've taken the bait – they're chasing the three prisoners."

"I hope they'll be okay," said Ajax, looking worried.

"Bah! Don't worry about them," said Cleaver. "They're all petty thieves – I'd say they spend half their lives running."

"And that's what we should be doing," said Quinn. "We need to get out of here."

"Right," said Cleaver. "Let's get Zain."

"You go and secure the *Libertas*," said Quinn, urgently. "We need to be ready to sail as soon as we hit the docks."

"Yes, sir," said Cleaver, with a half salute, and Quinn couldn't help but smile at the idea of the first mate taking orders from him.

"Ajax will carry the cleric down," said Quinn. "Ash can help me."

They stepped into the hallway to find Dilly easing the front door open and peering out. "They've all gone," he said, disbelief in his voice. "Even those guards who were fighting out in front. I don't think half of them even know who they're chasing."

"They don't need to know," said Ash, appearing from the front cell. "All they know is that it's not them, and they're glad of it."

"Ash," said Quinn, "I need you to help me get Zain ready to move."

She nodded.

"The rest of you – go and get the *Libertas* ready to sail. We'll follow as soon as we can."

The crew nodded as one, and Dilly, Abel, Ison and Cook disappeared out the door, followed by the remaining prisoner, who scuttled away looking relieved.

Ajax and Cleaver emerged from another cell, with the cleric suspended between them. "I'm okay," the old man said bravely, though his voice was feeble.

"You'll feel much better back in your own bed," said Ash.

Ajax smiled at Quinn. "I'll see you back in Verdania," he said firmly.

Quinn nodded, trying to return the smile, even as his mind whispered, *I hope.*

Chapter Fourteen

With the others gone, the prison was strangely silent. Quinn could hear his own breathing, and the scuffle of Ash's feet as she followed him down the hallway. They could still make out the baying of the crowd, and Quinn took comfort in the fact that the sound was moving away from them – which meant the three prisoners were still running.

Inside Zain's cell, Ash moved quickly, tearing strips from the bottom of Zain's white tunic and using them to bind his shoulder, which was still bleeding. "We really need to stitch this up," she said.

"There's no time for that!" snapped Quinn.

"I know," she snapped back. "I'm just saying. And just for that, you can do it when we get back to the *Libertas* – your sewing is neater than mine anyway!"

Quinn didn't argue with her. The time he'd spent alone with his mam, as the youngest son who was deemed too small for "real" farm work, had resulted in a very fine hand with a needle. He could also cook any one of her recipes, but he tried to keep that a secret.

"Is this the time for an argument?" Zain's sleepy, deep voice broke in.

"No," said Quinn. "But it is time to go. Are you done here, Ash?"

"She certainly is."

Quinn froze at the sound of the soft, menacing voice behind him. "Hello, Monstruo Mouse," it continued. "Surprised to see me?"

Quinn turned slowly to face Morpeth.

"Oh come now," he continued, leaning in the doorway. "You didn't think I'd fall for that ruse, did you? Let the rabble chase after whichever wolves it was you dressed up in sheep's clothing – leaving me to get the prize."

He paused, and Quinn could see his eyes taking in the prostrate form of Zain behind him. "Not much of a prize now, is it? I would have thought you'd put up more of a fight, Zain."

"You seem to have caught me on a bad day," said Zain, sounding breathless.

"No matter," said Morpeth. "It is the end result I am after, and I don't care how that's achieved."

"Have you told Forden about your ulterior motive?" asked Zain mildly.

Morpeth laughed, a harsh, ugly sound that was loud in the small cell. "He only wants to ensure that his map is the only complete map of the world," he said. "He cares nothing for you and your silly race. He will simply kill you all here in Deslond and be done with it. So if I kill you first, Zain, he will reward me handsomely. Whichever way you look at it, I win. Finally."

With that, he moved forward, shoving Quinn to one side so hard that he hit the wall with a crash.

"No!" shrieked Ash as Morpeth reached for Zain. She raked her nails across his face, doing her best to shove the big man off Zain.

"Why you –" Morpeth picked up Ash and threw her towards the door. She landed in a heap on the stone floor and was still.

"No!" Quinn shouted, crawling over the floor towards her, checking her over. A dark, ugly bruise was already appearing on the side of her face, but she was breathing and he could see her eyelids begin to flutter.

He turned back to Zain just in time to see him punch Morpeth in the face with all his might – which, unfortunately, was not as mighty as usual, given he was flat on his back and unable to hold Morpeth still with his injured arm.

"Ha!" said Morpeth, leaning back to avoid the worst of the blow, before punching Zain as hard as he could, directly on the injured shoulder. Zain's body seized with agony and then went limp. As Quinn watched, his arm flopped senselessly off the side of the sleeping platform, and Quinn knew he was out cold, the pain too much for him to take.

"The mighty Zain," Morpeth said, looking down with satisfaction at his vanquished foe. "Not so mighty now."

Filled with panic, Quinn stood. He knew it was up to him. If he, Zain and Ash were to get out of here, he needed to fight Morpeth – and win. But how?

"So, Monstruo Mouse, it comes to this. To you and to me."

Looking up into Morpeth's leering smile, Quinn could barely think and he could feel his muscles freeze from the feet up. If he didn't move soon, he wasn't going to be able to. He forced his weight from the back foot to the front, dancing up and down, trying to remind his body that it was a living thing, not a statue.

"Ah, so you want to dance, do you?" said Morpeth with glee. "Well, I suppose I have time for that."

Quinn watched in horror as the big man assumed the fighting stance, looking suddenly twice as big in the small space of the cell.

"You look worried, little mouse," said Morpeth, silkily. "I'll tell you what – to make it sporting, I'll throw this away." He dropped his knife to the floor, and Quinn's heart sank with it, knowing that Morpeth figured he could kill Quinn with his bare hands.

His mind raced, pulling together all his memories of Zain's careful training in the Deslondic fighting method, trying desperately to find something that might fit this situation.

"Stay on your feet."

"Keep your hands up."

None of those seemed enough.

As though of its own volition, his body began moving, ducking, weaving, dancing. And that's when Quinn knew that his one advantage was speed and agility. Morpeth stood still, arms up, awaiting an attack, but Quinn knew that if he went near the big man at this point, he would be flattened in seconds. But maybe, just maybe, if Quinn kept moving, he could tire his huge opponent to the point where Morpeth would make a mistake.

To do that, though, Quinn needed a bigger arena – this cell was simply too small for him to move around in.

He turned and ran out the door, positioning himself at the far end of the central room, the entrance behind him.

"Come, come, little mouse," said Morpeth, lumbering after him. "Leaving so soon?"

He barreled across the room towards Quinn, who forced himself to stand still until the last possible moment before jumping aside and ducking under Morpeth's outstretched arms. Morpeth crashed into the closed outside door, driven by the force of his own attack, as Quinn took himself across to the other side of the room.

"So, little mouse," said Morpeth, laughing maliciously as he turned to face Quinn again. "You want to play, do you?"

And so it began, with Quinn using every trick he could remember to stay out of Morpeth's reach, jiggling on the balls of his feet, ducking and weaving, constantly on the move, with Morpeth lunging after him. Quinn knew that if the Deslonder actually made contact with any of his swinging punches and kicks, Quinn would be knocked clear across the room – which was motivation enough to keep moving, moving, moving. He noted with gratitude that Morpeth's breath was coming in pants now and it seemed to him that his opponent was not as skilled as Zain – but that didn't make him less dangerous, and his threats became wilder and wilder.

"Bah!" gasped Morpeth eventually, his chest heaving. "Enough."

Quinn prepared for an attack, but to his horror Morpeth turned away from him and towards Zain's cell.

"Enough playing," the big man said, stumbling towards the door. "It is time to finish this. I know I said no weapons, but I have changed my mind."

"No!" shouted Quinn, realizing that Morpeth was going for his knife – and for Zain.

"Ha!" laughed Morpeth. "Such a clever Monstruo Mouse – but the man with the knife always wins." He turned to step through the door.

Quinn launched himself across the room, throwing his entire body at Morpeth's back, knocking him forward into the cell, and bringing them both to the ground with a crash, just a hand span from Ash's head.

Quinn had a moment to frown, realizing that Ash's body was not in the same position it had been when he'd left the cell, but then his attention was wholly taken up with the bucking, writhing body beneath him. Clutching the back of Morpeth's tunic, Quinn held on for dear life, knowing that if Morpeth managed to get on top of him, this fight would be all over and Quinn would be dead. Desperately, his eyes scanned the floor for the knife, but it was nowhere to be seen.

He shoved at the back of Morpeth's head, trying to push it to the stone floor with enough force to knock the man out, but it was like trying to hold on to his father's prized bull.

Suddenly, Morpeth let out a howl, rolling onto his side and clutching his ankle. The quick movement unseated Quinn and he fell to the floor with a thud, gasping as a loud crack rent the air accompanied by a piercing pain in his side.

He forced himself back up into a crouch, trying to ignore the fact that every breath was now torture. Morpeth's blood was trickling onto the floor and Quinn could see the Deslonder's own knife was buried deep in his ankle. Ash, white with fear, had moved into the corner, as far from the Deslonder's thrashing body as she could get.

"Good job," said Quinn. "Watch Zain."

She nodded, eyes wide, and pulled herself up onto the sleeping platform beside the still unconscious Zain. Quinn had never wished for anything so much as for his captain to wake up and tell him what to do.

But Morpeth was rousing himself, gripping the knife in two hands and pulling it from his ankle with a slurping sound and a fresh slick of blood. With a roar, he dragged himself to his feet and turned on Quinn, pure fury in his eyes. Quinn knew that he had to win this fight, or else . . .

Still crouching, trying to make himself as small a target as possible, Quinn struggled to stave off panic, knowing that only clear thinking would save them now.

Morpeth was moving towards him, knife raised, slipping in his own blood, howling like the banshees that Quinn's mam used to tell him about as a child. From his crouching position, Quinn watched him, wanting to close his eyes and have it all go away. Then he heard Zain's voice in his mind: "If a man cannot breathe, he cannot fight."

Quinn knew he would only get one chance at this and that he needed Morpeth to come close to make it work. Fighting every instinct in his body – which was telling him to run and never look back – he stayed crouched as Morpeth loomed closer and closer.

The Deslonder bent over him, chuckling cruelly. "And so it ends, Monstruo Mouse," he said. Morpeth raised the hand holding the knife and for a split second his chest enlarged and the soft flesh of his bull-like throat was visible.

Quinn launched himself upward, throwing all his weight behind his punch, and struck Morpeth on the neck, burying his fist in the man's windpipe.

The Deslonder's bellow died to a gurgle as he fell backward, landing with a thud on the cold stones. Quinn winced as Morpeth's head hit the stones with a sound like a squished melon, and then the Deslonder was still.

"Oh, Quinn, I think you've killed him," said Ash breathlessly.

Quinn shuddered, but then remembered the murderous look in Morpeth's eyes. "He would have killed us all," he replied with certainty. He crept over to look at the Deslonder, lying as still as the grave. But even as he watched, Morpeth's chest rose slightly.

"He's not dead," said Quinn. "We need to get out of here."

"How can we move Zain?" she asked. "He's out cold."

"We'll drag him if we have to," said Quinn. "But we're going now."

Between them, they managed to pull Zain from the bed, though Ash gasped when she saw the fresh blood staining his bandages as they did so.

"Quinn, we're hurting him," she cried.

"Yes, you are," came a deep voice at their feet.

"Zain! You're awake!"

Zain grimaced. "So it would seem," he said, looking around. "And it appears I have missed a great deal."

"We'll tell you all about it once we get to the *Libertas*," said Quinn, acutely aware that time was ticking away and that, any moment now, Forden might come in search of Morpeth. "Can you stand?"

"There is no question," said Zain slowly. "I must."

With a sigh of relief, Quinn watched as his captain pulled himself to his feet, swaying slightly, but upright nonetheless.

"Right, then," Quinn said with fake heartiness, "onward and upward."

Zain managed a laugh at the use of one of his favorite phrases. "Indeed," he said. "Let's go home."

Quinn frowned at Zain's use of the word "home," given that they were standing in the kingdom of his captain's birth, but decided that now was not the time to discuss it. That could wait. After all, they were still many weeks' sailing from Verdania – plenty of time for discussion.

With Zain leaning heavily and bleeding lightly on Ash and Quinn, they began the slow journey back to the docks.

Chapter Fifteen

Gritting his teeth, Quinn focused on counting steps. It was the only way to take his mind off the weight of Zain pressing down hard on his shoulder. He winced as he stumbled over a rock and his ribs protested. Quinn didn't think there was any part of him that wasn't black or blue or shades in between after his fights with Ira and then Morpeth. He readjusted his grip around Zain's broad back, grasping the big man's forearm tightly for balance.

Ash was also struggling, and he looked across to see that she had her eyes almost closed in concentration. Her dark hair was matted with Zain's blood, which continued to ooze from the wound in his shoulder.

A drop of water landed on Quinn's forehead and, as he had neither hand free to wipe it off, dripped off his nose – Zain was sweating in sheets, and it was this that kept Quinn's feet moving. If he was dragging himself along, how much worse was his captain feeling?

"Nearly there," he said.

"Oh, really? And I was so enjoying the walk," gasped Zain.

Ash managed a feeble laugh.

"Cleaver will be watching for us," said Quinn, eyes fixed on the end of the street. Just three more doors to pass and they would reach the corner and the safety of the docks. With any luck, the *Libertas* crew was on their way back now to help . . .

They stumbled forward and Quinn's heart gave a silent leap as they stepped from the shadows of the buildings and into the sunshine at the end of the dock. "Look," he said to Zain, pointing to the *Libertas*. "There!"

Zain looked up and nodded. "We've made it this far, we can get there."

Ash, looking exhausted, clenched her jaw and lifted her chin. "If you can, I can," she said.

All around them, sailors and deckhands went about their business, loading and unloading, leaning on boxes, shouting good-naturedly at each other, taking no notice of the trio. Strange things happened on the docks, and those who frequented them knew not to ask questions.

For Quinn, there was only the *Libertas*. Every step was taking them nearer, he knew – but why then did it still feel as though they were walking through his father's pig sty on a day after heavy rain?

"Well, well, well . . ." said a silky voice in Quinn's ear. "If it isn't Monstruo Mouse. I had not thought I'd see you again."

Quinn whirled around, earning a gasp from Zain, who wasn't up to quick movement.

Juan Forden stood in the shadow of a stack of boxes.

Fortunately, Zain's mind was working better than his body. "Mr. Forden," he said politely in Suspite.

"I am no mister," Forden replied in the same language. "I am Juan Forden, world's greatest explorer. And you are my prisoner."

Zain managed a smile at that. "I see," he said. "And yet . . ." He paused, looking around. "I see no ropes, no bars to hold me."

Forden roared with laughter. "Look at you!" he shrieked. "Bleeding all over the dock. You need no ropes or bars. You will soon be dead."

Quinn grimaced. There were altogether too many people talking offhandedly about Zain's death for his liking today. But, he had to concede, the current situation wasn't looking good for his captain – and it was up to Quinn to change that.

"Besides," Forden was continuing, "it is not you I want. You are no use to me. It is him." He pointed to Quinn. "You destroyed my ship," he said, conversationally. "Do you know how many pirates I had to kill to commandeer that pile of junk?" He gave a wild gesture in the direction of the pirate ship. Quinn had a sudden vision of the Golden Serpent's teeth glinting underwater as he disappeared to the bottom of the ocean, and shuddered. He was glad Egunon hadn't heard about that before they'd arrived at the Cave of Starstones, as he'd marked it on his map.

"And that was after we limped across several leagues of ocean in search of it. Oh no, little mouse, you owe me. I no longer have my beautiful ship, but I shall have you – and your map. I cannot return to Gelyn without it. Forden never loses."

"You will not take me," said Quinn calmly. There was no way he was going anywhere with Forden ever again.

"And you will do . . . what to stop me?" the Gelynion asked, twirling his moustache between his fingers, pretending to think, before drawing his sword. "You do not seem to understand, little mouse. I *cannot return* to Gelyn without the best map. The Queen does not offer second chances."

The world seemed to slow down as Quinn considered his options, taking in the sight of Forden, advancing towards him, step-by-step. Behind him, the sea glinted in the sunlight, beckoning Quinn – he would have given anything to be sailing on it right now, away from this place. He was exhausted, battered and sore, and he was supporting Zain, who would fall to the dock if Quinn left him.

Forden suddenly laughed out loud, startling a flock of seabirds, which rose as one screeching mass from the low wall of the dock behind him.

"What will you do?" he repeated, gleefully, like a man who knew he could not lose.

"I'll . . ." Quinn began, clutching for ideas.

"You'll step forward to meet him," Zain said in a low voice. "He doesn't want to kill you, Quinn Freeman. He needs you."

"You'll fall," Quinn answered from the side of his mouth. "And he doesn't need you – or Ash."

"Step forward to meet him," Zain repeated. "His sword is long. Get inside it."

Quinn gasped as he realized what his captain was saying – he wanted Quinn, unarmed, to put Forden in such a position that, to use his sword, he would need to move back. To make that happen, Quinn needed to be almost nose to nose with the Gelynion.

"Move forward, and keep moving."

It was an incredibly risky strategy but, Quinn thought wearily, his only choice.

And so he moved suddenly, leaving Zain to shift all his weight onto Ash's slender shoulders, and thrust himself forward, inside the range of Forden's sword.

The Gelynion grunted, taking an instinctive step back. Quinn moved again, hustling Forden, not allowing him the room to take a swing, drawing one hand back as though to punch. The Gelynion would never know that he didn't even have enough strength to swat a fly at that point – his training meant that his posture looked strong.

Again Forden retreated, trying to find the room to bring his weapon about, making feeble striking motions that Quinn was easily able to avoid. Relentlessly he advanced, shrieking his frustration and anger at the Gelynion, gaining strength from his own fury. Now Quinn raised both arms above his head, waving them about, creating as much commotion as he could. He felt, rather than saw, the crowd that began to gather around them, shouting support for what they perceived to be the underdog – the small boy facing down a fully grown man with a sword.

Forden, used to fawning admiration, faltered in the face of the crowd's disapproval, and Quinn pressed home his advantage, pushing closer and closer, even reaching down and trying to take hold of the handle of Forden's sword.

The Gelynion swore. "Enough!" he roared, taking a huge step back to make some room. "This ends now!"

As he swung the sword back to strike, the booing and cursing of the crowd swelled. Quinn glanced around, wondering what his next step would be, wondering if any of these onlookers would choose to stop watching and actually help him. As he did so, Quinn suddenly knew exactly where he was.

"Yes," he said simply to Forden. "It does." With that, he drew on every reserve of strength he had and threw himself forward, thrusting both hands at the Gelynion's soft middle, and hoping for the best. He heard the whistle as the raised sword swung towards him – and then the soft "*oof*" as Forden's legs ran into the low wall on the edge of the dock.

Hours of training had given Quinn the ability to change direction on a centime, and he used his last remaining strength to do that now, throwing himself sideways and landing in a heap.

He turned to watch as, arms windmilling, the Gelynion fell backward over the wall. Quinn could see the look of panic and confusion in his eyes as he disappeared over the side with a huge, graceless splash.

Breathing hard, Quinn lay still, listening to the Gelynion's screams for help.

"Nice work," said a voice above him.

Quinn looked up to see Ajax staring down at him.

"Where did you come from?" Quinn spluttered. "I thought you were going back to the *Fair Maiden*."

"I was," Ajax said, laughing. "But Cleaver and the others needed some help, er, liberating the *Libertas* from the three guards left on board, which took some time. I was just on my way back to the *Fair Maiden* when I saw the crowd and came over to see what was happening."

"Just in time to see that last move of yours," added Tomas, appearing beside him, supporting Zain on one side, while a valiant, white-lipped Ash still stood at the other.

"The *Libertas!*" exclaimed Quinn. "How is she?" He had sudden visions of the ship being ransacked and pillaged, or worse.

"In surprisingly good shape," said Tomas. "We've lost bits and pieces of furniture and most of our supplies, but you know, she doesn't look like much. I think they thought we had nothing to steal. Most of the cabins have been tossed, but there's no major damage."

Quinn once again blessed his captain for his choice of the solid, utilitarian craft, and thanked the stars that "no damage" in the cabins meant that the hidey-holes hadn't been discovered.

"And the map?" he asked. He didn't really care about the state of the false map, left under the floorboard, not now that he knew his real one, in the cleric's cabin, was safe. But he had to ask.

"Sorry, Quinn, but they've made a mess of your cabin. Ink spilled everywhere, floorboards pulled up, and the map is missing."

Quinn nodded, and tried to look as though he cared. "I can do it again," he said reassuringly, looking at Zain. And he could – it made no difference whatsoever if that map was accurate.

"We have to go," Ash prompted. "We need to get out of here, away from this place. Where is that horrible man?"

Quinn crawled to the edge of the dock, scanning the water. Forden was clinging for dear life to one of the poles supporting the dock and Quinn had a sudden perfect memory of a meeting in Forden's cabin: "Yergon is very proud of the fact that he's the *only* man aboard the *Black Hawk* who can swim . . . let him prove it."

Yergon was Forden's mapmaker, and Quinn had saved him from a watery grave that day.

As though the memory had conjured him up, the little man appeared beside the Verdanians, staring down at his captain in the water below.

"Hello, Monstruo," he said in Gelynion, settling down on the dock next to Quinn on the low rail. Quinn realized that the other mapmaker had never heard his real name.

"It is good to see you," he said to Yergon sincerely. He had been worried about the mapmaker since he'd last seen him on the deck of the *Black Hawk*.

Yergon nodded, and they both stared back at the quivering wreck that was Juan Forden.

"Are you going to save him?" Quinn asked in Gelynion, wondering what Yergon, who had suffered at Forden's hands, would do.

Yergon looked across at Quinn and smiled. "Oh yes," he said, shyly. Then he paused, before adding, with a twinkle in his eye, "In a little while."

Quinn let go of Zain's arm long enough to clap Yergon on the back. "Good luck," he said. "And thank you."

"For what?" the Gelynion asked.

"For what you did on the ship," said Quinn. "I wouldn't have gotten off the *Black Hawk* without you."

"And I," said Yergon, "wouldn't have stayed on the *Black Hawk* without you. I'd say that makes us even."

Down below, Forden had gotten over the shock of his unexpected dunking and was now shrieking at Yergon to "do something."

Yergon sighed. "I suppose I'd better get him out of there," he said, removing his boots. "With any luck we can be back on board before Morpeth reappears." Quinn knew that Yergon had about as much love for the huge Deslonder as Quinn himself did.

"I, er, think he'll be a while," Quinn ventured. "Last time I saw him, he was . . . resting in a jail cell."

Yergon gave him a long look. "Hmm," he said. "Perhaps you go one up on me again."

With that, he sighed and stood, before executing a perfect dive into the water.

"Come on," said Quinn, moving back to his friends. "I think the show's over. Let's go home."

"Good idea," said Ajax, stirring beside him. "Odilon will be wondering where I am – and I don't want to be left here on the dock."

"There will always be a place for you on the *Libertas*," Zain rumbled. "Always."

Ajax blushed. "Yes, well . . . I'll see you in Verdania," he said, reaching over to grasp Zain's hand.

Zain winced. "Indeed," he said. "May the best ship win."

It was a sobering reminder that they were competitors and that the hour of reckoning was drawing nearer. Looking at the blood still dripping from Zain's shoulder as they turned to hobble towards their ship, Quinn could only hope they all made it home.

Chapter Sixteen

"And so we commit his body to the sea – may he rest in peace now and forever," said Cleaver, as Abel and Ison took the body, wrapped tightly in a quilt and lifted it up and over the rail of the *Libertas*.

Quinn swallowed a sob at the sound of the faint splash that followed.

"How could this happen?" Ash wailed. "This wasn't supposed to happen. I tried so hard to save him."

Quinn put a comforting arm around her shaking shoulders. She was shivering as though freezing, in spite of the heat of the day. "There was nothing you could do," he said, wiping away his own tears.

"I didn't do enough," she cried, as her dignity crumbled and she leaned against him for support. "Not enough."

Tomas came to her other side, putting an arm around her waist to help Quinn hold her up. "Come on, Ash," he said, "I'll take you down to Quinn's cabin for a rest."

Quinn watched as Tomas led Ash away, hobbling like an old lady. She'd been up the entire night before, trying every healing salve she knew and some she'd made up on the spot, but nothing had worked.

The gentle cleric was gone.

Quinn couldn't believe it was only yesterday afternoon that he'd been thinking that maybe, just maybe, all their troubles were finally over.

Quinn, Ash, Zain and Tomas had made it back to the *Libertas* just as the sun was setting over the ocean, turning it orange and gold, and every one of those last few steps had seemed to take an age.

Fortunately, Jericho had seen Forden's dunking and had run down with Abel to greet their captain, taking his weight just as they all heard shouts behind them. Turning, Quinn saw that the angry Deslondic crowd had arrived, and was charging down the pier towards them with a throaty, deafening roar.

Quinn had not known he could move so fast, grabbing Ash by the hand and dragging her behind him as he flew with Tomas towards the ship's gangplank. Jericho and Abel were stumbling under the weight of Zain but they, too, were moving at superhuman speed.

Ash ran lightly up the gangplank and Quinn stepped aside to let Jericho and Abel go ahead of him – they had to turn sideways to carry Zain to the deck and Quinn put all his weight behind pushing at Abel's side, trying to help them to keep their balance. At last, they were safely on board, and Ison was pulling up the gangplank behind them as Dilly cast off the ropes that held the *Libertas* to the dock.

Abel had all but dumped Zain on deck in his haste to get to the strong pole in the bow that they used to push the *Libertas* away from dangerous rocks, shoving it over the side and levering the ship away from the pier.

"Help me!" he shouted to Dilly, who ran to join him.

"We need to do the stern as well," yelled Quinn, noticing that the ship was moving outward in an arc – the bow was leaving the dock, but the stern was moving closer at the same time.

"Hold fast," Abel shouted, as he and Dilly raced to the other end of the ship.

"Hoist the sails," Cleaver ordered, and Quinn ran to the mast, shinnying up and unfurling billowing sails behind him as he went, praying they'd catch some wind to carry the *Libertas* to safety.

Around him, the sails flapped as the gentle breeze swirled around them. Under normal circumstances, they'd have towed the ship out using a rope from the longboat, guiding her to the open water.

But these were not normal circumstances.

Then Quinn felt the breeze lift his hair and he whooped as the sails ballooned. "We've done it," he shouted, clutching the mast as he nearly swooned with relief. "We're moving!"

A triangle of white water appeared at the *Libertas*'s bow as she began to plow through the harbor, creating a swell that rocked the boats at anchor around them. Cleaver was going to have to steer very carefully if they were to make it out of here under full sail without hitting anything.

Quinn glanced back at the dock, which was slowly melting away from them. Juan Forden was standing on the end of the pier, water dripping from his luxuriant moustache, shouting in Gelynion. Quinn thought it was probably a good thing he couldn't quite make out what Forden was saying – it might give him several choice phrases that his mam would not like one little bit.

He gasped as he saw a group of Deslondic men jump into the dragon boat that was still tied near where the *Libertas* had been docked. He had seen how swift the smaller boats were – and how deadly those arrows could be.

But the men seemed to be arguing with each other, screaming and yelling, getting in each other's way as they tried to hoist the sail and, with every moment that passed, the *Libertas* pulled farther away. Still, he slid back down the mast to report what he'd seen to Cleaver.

"They won't catch us now," the old salt said confidently, wiping his brow with his red bandanna. Quinn's eyes widened when he saw how bald Cleaver was underneath that bandanna – he'd never before seen the man without it!

"We'll continue under full sail through the night," Cleaver went on. "North. It's time we went home."

He had assumed the role of captain, and it jolted Quinn. He'd been so caught up in the escape that he'd forgotten all about Zain, last seen lying in a bloody heap on the deck.

"Where's Zain?" Quinn asked fearfully.

"In his cabin, resting," said Cleaver. Then, seeming to notice Quinn's distress, he reached over and grasped his shoulder. "He'll be okay," he said. "He's tougher than he looks."

Even Quinn managed a wry smile at this attempt at a joke, and he left Cleaver chortling.

Down in Zain's cabin, he found Ash cleaning the arrow wound with fresh water, and frowning.

"How is it?" he asked her.

"Wouldn't you like to ask me?" Zain said.

"Oh, right, yes," said Quinn, embarrassed.

Zain smiled and Quinn had never been happier to see the baring of those teeth. "It is painful," said Zain, "but much better than it was when I was locked in that cell. Thanks to you and Ash."

Quinn looked at his feet, blushing. "Well, you would have done the same for us," he said.

Zain lay back on his pillow and laughed out loud. "Indeed, Quinn Freeman," he said. "Indeed."

"I hope you brought your best sewing hand with you," said Ash, looking up from her task.

Quinn gulped. "I was hoping it wouldn't come to that," he admitted, running suddenly sweaty hands over his patched breeches. It was true he'd spent hours stitching them back together after his run-in with the *pescarn* – but he didn't think that sewing up Zain would be quite the same.

"Well, it has," she said, handing him a needle and thread. "If we don't stitch up the wound it won't heal. Do your mam proud."

He took the needle, and looked at Zain anxiously.

"Do not fear," said Zain. "Even you couldn't hurt me more than an arrow through the shoulder. But make it neat. I don't want to frighten my daughter when I get home."

"No pressure then," said Quinn, trying to make light of it.

"None at all," said Zain.

"I'll leave you to it," said Ash brightly, edging towards the door.

"Aren't you staying?" asked Quinn, horrified.

"Oh no," she said gaily. "I can't stand the sight of needles in flesh."

With that, she was gone, leaving Quinn, the needle and thread, and Zain.

Quinn pulled a chair closer to the bed and picked up the candle. "You'll need to hold this with your other hand," he told Zain. "There's not much light in here."

Zain nodded, taking it from him.

Quinn threaded the needle, as his mam had shown him, and tied a knot in the end. "Right," he said. "Here goes then."

Taking a calming breath, he pushed the sharp needle into one side of the open wound. Zain gasped, and the candle flickered as he moved involuntarily.

"Talk to me, Quinn Freeman," he ordered. "I need distracting."

Feeling slightly ill at the sight of the thread pulling through skin, Quinn decided that he needed distracting, too.

"Okay," he said, pulling the thread across the wound and pushing the needle through the other side. "I . . . that is . . . you –"

"*Leif's boots!*" grunted Zain, as the needle flashed into the wound again. "Is there something on your mind?"

And so Quinn found himself outlining Morpeth's accusations and the reaction of the mob.

Zain kept perfectly still as Quinn told him how Morpeth had labeled him a traitor and Verdanian spy, exhaling sharply as Quinn recalled, word for word, Morpeth's story.

"He was, er, very convincing," said Quinn.

There was silence.

"And were you convinced?"

Quinn stopped sewing, looking up into Zain's pained eyes. "No," he said, truthfully. "I wasn't. But . . ."

"But?" asked Zain. Quinn noticed that he didn't even raise one eyebrow.

"I didn't tell the others," Quinn said, nodding upstairs. "I didn't want . . . well . . ."

"You thought that others might not be so willing to discount Morpeth's story," said Zain.

"It's just that – it's been clear all along that you and Morpeth hate each other," said Quinn in a rush, focusing once again on the needle sliding in and out of Zain's flesh.

Zain sighed. "Once upon a time, Morpeth and I were like brothers," he admitted. "But times change." He lapsed into silence once more, and Quinn thought he was going to hear no more.

Quinn realized that his length of thread was too short to do the entire wound, which was wider than he'd thought. He tied it off, and moved to Zain's desk, where Ash had left a bowl of water, cleaning the needle before rethreading it.

As the needle pierced the skin once more, Zain seemed to come back from wherever he'd gone in his mind. "I will tell you the story of Morpeth and me and how we came to be . . . the way we are," he said. "It is a story of love and a story of hatred – and how close those two things can be."

Quinn nodded, not daring to speak.

"Morpeth and I grew up together in Mendoree, a small village not an hour's walk from Fesna. It was a beautiful place, near a natural water hole – a rare thing in Deslond."

Quinn managed a smile, noticing the faraway look in Zain's eyes.

"Our fathers were the best of friends. My father was chief of our village, and Morpeth's father his closest advisor. But Morpeth's parents were killed in a cart accident when he was just three years old. My parents took Morpeth in, and raised us as brothers. We spent all our time together and shared everything."

"When we were sixteen, a new family moved to the village, bringing their daughter Hadiya with them. Morpeth and I both fell in love with her at first sight. But she chose me." Even as he winced in pain from his wound, Zain smiled at the memory. "Morpeth never forgave me for it," he continued. "But Hadiya and I married just two years later and we were happy."

Quinn tried to imagine being married in just four years' time, but decided that he'd just concentrate on his stitching instead.

"It wasn't until the wedding that I realized the true strength of Morpeth's resentment," said Zain thoughtfully.

"It was as though Hadiya was a prize and he had come second. He disappeared that night."

Quinn thought back to Morpeth's words to Zain in that dark Deslondic cell. *"I win. Finally."*

"Did he always come second?" he asked Zain.

Zain closed his eyes. "You are beginning to see, Quinn Freeman. Yes, he did, but always so closely."

Quinn thought about how he felt when he was constantly bested by his brother Allyn. "And did you, er, remind him of that fact?" he asked Zain.

Zain sighed. "I was so young," he said. "Yes, of course I did. But to me, it was healthy competition. I took great pride in besting him because it was always such a close contest. I truly admired him. I did not think about what it would be like to be him, to never come out on top."

The big man closed his eyes as he considered it now. "Unfortunately, it ate away at him. I wish I had known . . ." Zain's face was grim. "Three months after the wedding, Verdania invaded Deslond," said Zain. "At least, that's what it looked like to us. King Orel has since explained to me that he was invited to Deslond for diplomatic talks and his ships came under attack as he arrived. It seems our emperor had designs on building a bigger empire and had lured King Orel in to kill him, but none of that was clear at the time."

Quinn shook his head. He'd read about the Crusadic Wars in the books that his local cleric had lent him, but the beginnings were shrouded in mist, even to the record keepers.

"As the chief's son, it was up to me to defend our village," said Zain. "My father was getting older, and so I gathered the young men together and off we went to battle – at first full of hope and bravado, thinking it was a great adventure, but . . . there is nothing fun about war."

Zain lapsed into silence again, and Quinn took the opportunity to finish his stitches, tying off the thread, and sitting back to admire his handiwork.

"Anyway," said Zain, shaking his head as though to clear it. "I did . . . quite well and my reputation grew and grew."

Quinn remembered some of the stories the other crew members had told him about Zain's exploits in battle, about his fearsome reputation and his legendary leadership, and concluded that "quite well" meant "extraordinarily well."

"And Morpeth?" asked Quinn.

"I did not know if he was alive or dead," said Zain. "I looked for him in every battle. I still missed him, you see – he could have been a great commander, too, and I could have used his help. The war dragged on and on. Then, one night, I received a message from my father – I was needed at home."

Quinn wasn't sure if he wanted to hear the rest.

"I got there to find that I was too late. My village had been razed to the ground and everyone, Hadiya and my mother and father included, was dead."

Quinn gasped, trying to imagine what that would feel like.

"Imagine my surprise when Morpeth appeared in the ruins of the village, eyes full of tears, to tell me it was Verdanians who had done it," said Zain. "I was so overcome with rage and anger and horror that I did not care if I lived or died. And so I rode like a madman right into the Verdanian camp, taking my horse straight into the tent where King Orel was holding a war council."

He smiled ruefully. "How I was not killed, I will never know," he said. "Perhaps the cleric's god was with me that day."

Quinn said nothing, waiting to hear what came next.

"King Orel is very brave," said Zain. "Confronted with the sight of a raging, swearing Deslonder swinging a sword, he invited me to sit down and take tea with him."

Quinn laughed out loud, and Zain's face twisted in a lopsided smile. "Indeed. I was so surprised, I could only agree. And that's when he told me that his army had, that very morning, captured a band of rogue Deslondic army deserters who were boasting about having destroyed a village, as though that would bolster their chances of release."

Quinn gasped again.

"Of course, I demanded to see these men, to question them, and Orel took me to them. They thought that I could secure their release and so they told me everything. They'd been set up by a man named Morpeth, who'd instructed them to ransack Mendoree. It would be easy, he'd said, because there were no young men there. They were to wear masks, round everyone up and lock them in the central building before taking what they wanted – as long as they allowed him to step in after an allocated time to 'rescue' the villagers."

Even now, Zain's fists clenched at the thought. "He wanted to be a hero," he said, voice flat. "He wanted to save the village and show them all – show Hadiya – what he was made of, while I wasn't there. But it all went wrong. The women and the old men put up more of a fight than anyone could ever have expected, ripping away the masks, and then . . . the gang panicked. They locked everyone in the central building and set fire to it, trying to cover their tracks."

Zain swallowed. "From what I heard, Morpeth did his best to put the fire out, but he was one man and it moved too quickly, taking out the whole village."

"They all died?"

"Every one," said Zain.

"But . . . why does Morpeth blame you?"

Zain shook his head. "Think on what I have told you, Quinn Freeman. The answer lies there."

Quinn thought quickly, flashing back through the story. Zain's words: "Then, one night, I received a message from my father – I was needed at home." And then: "The gang panicked."

"They heard you were coming," he said, slowly. "They heard you were on the way and that's what made them panic."

Zain's sigh was long and painful. "My father saw them approaching and sent the fastest rider in the village to find me. He knew I was not far away, for I had sent word that I was hoping to visit soon. Unfortunately, I suspect he told the gang, hoping that the threat would be enough to make them leave . . ."

His words trailed away, before he roused himself once more. "In Morpeth's twisted mind, it's my fault. If it hadn't been for me, he would never have been put in the position of trying to prove himself. If it hadn't been for me, it would never have gone wrong. I have no doubt that it has torn him apart over the years, because it has torn me apart too. To think that my youthful disregard could have created such a . . . monster. And Morpeth blames me because it is easier than admitting the truth to himself."

Quinn could see how it could burn away at a person's insides until they were no longer whole. He was also beginning to see why Zain never discussed his prowess as a great army leader. As far as Zain was concerned, his reputation had killed his family.

"I don't really understand why you didn't simply kill him when you first saw him in Kurt's village," said Quinn.

"I have seen enough killing in my life," said Zain simply. "Besides, sometimes being allowed to live with what we have done is a far more painful punishment."

Quinn let that lie. Bringing up Kurt's name had brought another question. "You lost your village – like Kurt did. That's why you went easy on him."

Zain sighed. "Yes," he admitted. "I can see the awful battle in him. The questions he is asking himself, the terrible void that is created when you have no roots. It reminds me of those early days after . . ." His voice trailed away. "But," Zain said suddenly. "I think that perhaps I was wrong about Kurt – I gave him too much leeway."

Quinn grimaced, wanting to shout "YES!" Kurt had not been seen since his hasty exit from the Deslondic jail. Jericho and Cleaver reported that he'd scarpered off down the road in the direction of the *Libertas*, running ahead as fast as he could. By the time they'd reached the ship, Kurt had gone – along with most of the contents of the starstone sack. Quinn suspected he'd taken as many handfuls as he could fit in his pockets. He could only be grateful that the Deslonders hadn't recognized the rest for what they were.

"Where do you think he went?" Quinn asked Zain now. In Quinn's best-case scenario, Kurt was stranded on the docks in Deslond – but he knew the other boy was too sly for that.

"I suspect we have not seen the last of Kurt," was all Zain would say.

"Well, you're all sewn now," said Quinn, taking the candle from Zain. "I'll get Ash back in to put some healing salve on it and rebandage you."

Zain reached over with his good hand to grasp Quinn's arm. "Thank you, Quinn Freeman," he said. "Your mam would be proud."

Quinn managed a smile. "I'm not sure she had this in mind when she taught me to sew," he said.

Zain laughed. "Maybe not."

"Er, before I go . . ."

"Yes?"

"I just . . . don't understand how you came to be a slave?"

Zain fell back against his pillows once more. "Ah yes, that."

Quinn waited.

"I was reeling from the revelations about Morpeth, when King Orel asked me to help him end the war," said Zain, voice distant as though picturing the scene. "I agreed. After everything that had happened . . . there are no winners in war, not really. There is just death and destruction on both sides, and one side loses more. So I agreed to go to the emperor as King Orel's translator and help to negotiate a peace. It wasn't easy and it took months and months, and what I saw in my emperor during those negotiations made me realize that I could no longer live in Deslond, not while he was ruling. He would not have allowed it. So I asked King Orel to take me with him."

"But you asked, so why . . . ?"

Zain looked at him sadly. "There is no place in Verdania for a Deslondic man other than as a servant," he said. "The King explained that to me and suggested that I go somewhere else and start afresh, but where would I go? I'd lost my home, my family. King Orel was a decent man and I thought that his kingdom would be a good place to live. And so I agreed to act as his slave."

He raised his eyes to Quinn. "Verdania has been good to me in many ways," he said. "I met Sia, my wife, in the palace kitchens, after she arrived with a shipload of Deslondic refugees, fleeing the reign of the emperor. I will never forget Hadiya, and my family, but I have been able to build a different life there, with King Orel's help."

Quinn remembered his impressions of the relationship between the King and Zain, that they were more friends than master and slave. He had been right. "But now you're in the race?"

"The one legitimate way for the King to set me 'free' and then find a role for me in the palace is if I earn it," said Zain. "This is the only way. I confess, for a time, that I did wonder if I might take my family back to Deslond, that it would be different now. But I have been 'home' and it felt more foreign to me than any of the unknown lands we have visited."

"So the story about you being a traitor . . ."

"Just a story, Quinn Freeman. A way for Morpeth to raise the blood pressure of a crowd to boiling point. Always remember that your reaction to any story depends very much on who is telling it – and what they choose to reveal."

He closed his eyes, and Quinn could almost feel the sadness seeping from him.

"I am tired now," said Zain.

Quinn stood up and crept from the room, expecting Ash to be outside the door.

Instead, he'd found Tomas. "You have to go and help Ash," he said, eyes wild. "It's the cleric! He's taken a turn for the worse."

Chapter Seventeen

Now, his eyes red and sore from crying, Quinn couldn't believe that less than a day had passed. The cleric, already weak from his illness, had been unable to cope with the stress of the flight from the jail, and had collapsed on board the *Libertas*. Each member of the crew had been in to visit, though the old man wasn't talking much by the time Quinn got to him.

"You must tell Zain about your map," he'd gasped. "I have written to the King of the other one."

Quinn had nodded, trying to hush the old man. "Save your strength," he murmured, wondering how the cleric had held a quill.

The cleric had laughed, a husky, wheezy sound. "Even if I gathered it into a bag, it wouldn't amount to much."

After that, he'd lapsed into a fitful sleep, and Quinn had sat with him a few more minutes before stealing out.

"What did he say to you?" he'd asked Ash later.

"He kept saying 'look up,'" she said, frowning. "I looked up but all I could see was ceiling. I asked him what he meant, but he'd gone back to sleep. I'll ask him again later."

But there was no later. "Look up" turned out to the cleric's last words, and now his earthly remains had been committed to the sea.

Slumped in a corner of the stern, watching as the crew morosely went about their work, Quinn felt hollow. "It wasn't supposed to turn out like this." Those had been Ash's words and he couldn't help but agree.

He hadn't wanted to come on this journey, but he'd done the right thing by his family and given his best, as he'd promised he would. He'd imagined terrible things happening to him – sailing over the edge of the world, the fire-breathing jaws of Genesi – but he'd never figured on loss.

He stretched out on his stomach on the deck, face-down in his arms. Even considering pirates, kidnapping, robbery, sea monsters and all the rest – he had never wanted to be home as much as he did right now.

"Are you okay, Quinn?" Tomas dropped down beside him, placing his hand on Quinn's back.

"Go away," mumbled Quinn.

There was a short silence, but the hand remained. "I know it hurts," Tomas began. "I hurt, too."

"You didn't know him as well as I did," Quinn shot back, turning over to sit upright.

"No," agreed Tomas. "But you don't have to be an old friend to be a good friend. The cleric helped me a lot."

"With what?"

"Just . . . listening," said Tomas.

Quinn nodded. Cleric Greenfield had been good at that.

"Anyway, I was thinking . . ."

Quinn waited.

"I'm sorry about your map," said Tomas, in a rush. They weren't sure whether it was the Deslonders or Kurt who had taken the map from Quinn's cabin, though Quinn had his suspicions – after all, Deslondic fishermen were highly unlikely to have even recognized the map for what it was, let alone looked under the floorboards for it.

Quinn was silent, thinking about the tricky conversation that he still needed to have with Zain about the real map.

"I think you should start again," said Tomas. "Do it for the cleric, Quinn. Win it for him. He believed in you so much."

Quinn was silent.

"The only way to make all of this – any of it – worthwhile is to win the race," said Tomas. "None of us can do it without you."

Quinn nodded slowly. Tomas was right. All of it came down to him now. They were in a headlong flight for the finish line, trying to make it back by the last day of their allocated year. Cleaver had admitted it was touch and go. They knew where they were now, so he had an idea of approximately how long it would take to get back to Verdania – and Cleaver admitted that they'd need the winds to be with them every single day if they were to make it.

But after that, it all came down to the map. Which meant it all came down to Quinn.

If nothing else, it would take his mind off things. He truly became lost in his own world when he was with his map. He was proud of the color, the beautiful gilt details he'd added to the banners, and the fine line work of the navigation markers.

"I'll go now," he said, dragging himself to his feet. But he wasn't about to start fresh. Instead, he would collect the real map from the cleric's empty cabin – even the thought threatened to bring fresh tears – and give it the attention it deserved.

Then, of course, he'd show it to Zain . . . He swallowed nervously at the thought of telling his captain he'd been keeping the map from him all these many long moon cycles.

If that conversation didn't distract him from his yearning for home, nothing would . . .

Chapter Eighteen

The moon was sulking behind gray clouds, casting the palest of light as the *Libertas* slid quietly into the harbor at Oakston. The gloomy silence was broken only by the splish-splash of water on her bow, and the docks were dark and deserted.

It wasn't quite how Quinn had imagined their homecoming to be. But then, the last time he'd seen this port, he'd been thinking he wouldn't get home at all.

The cold silvery light waxed and waned with the movement of the clouds, casting shadows over the familiar landscape. There was the harbormaster's cottage and the market square. High on the hill, the dark silhouette of King Orel's castle loomed over the whole town.

And there, bobbing alongside the pier in the gentle waves created by the *Libertas*'s entrance, were the *Fair Maiden* and the *Wandering Spirit*, looking settled and confirming Quinn's worst fears.

Quinn pulled his cloak closer around him, one hand creeping up to grab the lucky tooth that hung around his neck – and coming away empty. He hadn't seen it since he'd used it to open Zain's door in the Deslondic jail, and he missed it sorely.

He sighed, thinking about how unlucky they'd been without the tooth – and Nammu, who hadn't been sighted since her rescue.

The winds had not been with them. It was as though the cleric's death took the very breath from the earth and the *Libertas* had limped up the coast from Deslond. Quinn had hoped against hope that the other two ships had met the same conditions, that there was still a chance that the *Libertas* would somehow triumph, entering Oakston harbor first.

As it turned out, they were last. And they were late. All on board the *Libertas* had watched helplessly as the days left in their one-year deadline had ticked away, until, finally, their date of return had passed – while they were still one day from home.

Quinn's fists clenched. To have been so close and to have missed out . . .

The only thing that could save them now was Quinn's map. It had to be so extraordinary, so outstanding, that King Orel would overlook the small matter of that missed deadline . . .

He felt a hand on his shoulder.

"Well, Quinn Freeman, we made it," said Zain. His wound had healed beautifully over the past few weeks, and Ash had taken some comfort from that. She still blamed herself for the loss of the cleric despite reassurances from the rest of the crew.

"We did," said Quinn. "But too late."

"Maybe so," said Zain. "Yet there was a time when you would have been happy just to be back at all."

Quinn managed a wry grin. "True," he said. "I just –"

"I know," said Zain. "To go so far and then . . . but do not give up hope. There is still a chance. I cannot see how your map will be beaten."

Quinn had finally confessed the existence of his "real" map to Zain. With Kurt gone, there was no reason not to do so. After berating him soundly for keeping secrets, Zain had finally admitted that it may have been a good thing. At least Kurt hadn't given away the true secrets of Quinn's map when he'd stolen it in Tomas's homeland, Barbarin, nor, as suspected, taken the almost complete fake map in Deslond.

"I didn't expect it to be so . . ."

"Quiet," finished Zain. "No. Somehow you feel that the docks should be lined with people clapping and screaming."

"Well, at least my mam and da," admitted Quinn.

"But how could they know?" asked Zain, gently.

Quinn swallowed. He couldn't help but feel that it was all horribly . . . anticlimactic. To have sailed around the known and unknown world, to have escaped pirates, "sea monsters" and knife-wielding Gelynions; to have discovered new lands and new people and new plants . . . And then to come back to a deserted dock and the knowledge that you'd missed the boat, so to speak.

"Come, Quinn," said Zain. "The crew is preparing to dock. If nothing else, we shall sleep in soft, comfortable beds, with full bellies and warm fires tonight."

Quinn nodded.

"You might even attempt a hot bath," Zain continued, poking him playfully in the ribs. "You probably won't want to meet your mam smelling quite as savory as you do."

Quinn laughed. "While you, of course, smell like Queen Lorelei's lavender plants."

"Frankly, you both reek like dead horses," came a voice behind them.

"Ah, my little stowaway," said Zain, turning to face Ash. "Always so diplomatic."

Ash laughed.

"I'm glad you're here," Zain continued. "You've just reminded me that we are very close to seeing that book Quinn told us about."

"Book?" queried Quinn, without thinking.

"Why yes," said Zain, eyes dancing. "Remember. The one that proves that females on ships are not bad luck.

The entire crew is waiting to hear that passage you and Ash talked about."

Quinn gulped. The truth was, he'd made that up on the first day that Ash had been discovered on the *Libertas* – anything to keep Zain and the others from following the myths of the sea and throwing her overboard.

"Oh," he began. "About that . . ."

Ash's eyes were huge.

"Yes," said Zain politely, eyebrow raised.

"Remember Ash and I told you I'd been having some trouble with my memory after that bump on the head on the *Black Hawk*," said Quinn, scrabbling for words.

"Yes," said Zain. "The trouble you concealed from me." Just another thing he was still grumpy about.

"Well, er," Quinn stalled.

"His memory came back," said Ash, jumping in, "but there are still some sketchy patches."

Zain rolled his eyes to the distant moon. "Don't tell me," he said. "The one thing that Quinn Freeman cannot remember is the exact details of that particular book."

"That's right!" said Quinn in relief. "That's exactly right. The one thing."

Zain laughed. "Never take any job that requires you to lie, Quinn Freeman. You are not good at it."

With that, he walked away, chuckling to himself, leaving Quinn to wonder if he'd *ever* actually believed the story about the book.

"That went well," said Ash uncertainly, and Quinn knew she was wondering, too.

"No matter," he said. "We made it, Ash. Around the world." He had a fleeting memory of Egunon mentioning those mysterious chiefs "to the east" and the rumors of southern lands, and wondered briefly about that, before shaking it off. They'd mapped the known world, and that was that.

"And back again," said Ash, staring ahead as the stone buildings of Oakston grew larger.

"What will you do now?" he asked her. "Mam will want you to come home with us."

Ash turned to look at him, and he could see the glint of tears in her eyes. "I can't go back to Markham," she said, as he'd told Tomas she would. "Not after what happened."

She turned back to face the looming town. "No, I'll stay in the castle – I'll take my new plants to the garden. I'm sure they'll find a place for me."

"Zain will help you," said Quinn.

She sighed. "If we'd won, he might have been able to do that," she said. "But . . ." Her voice trailed away.

Quinn had told no one about his conversation with Zain, and the truth behind his captain's relationship with the King, knowing it was something that Zain would not want him to talk about. "He won't let you down," he said now to Ash. "No matter what happens with the race."

She nodded. "He'll do his best, I know."

After that, there was nothing more to do but to stand in the moonlight beside each other and watch as the *Libertas* sailed into shore.

Home.

Quinn could only hope their luck might change now they were back.

Chapter Nineteen

It wasn't supposed to end like this.

"I'm sorry, Zain," the King was saying. "It's just too different. The other two have so many similarities – all I can think is that your mapmaker got it wrong."

Quinn wanted to scream, but he didn't think he'd be heard in the crowded counting house. The only reason the other two maps were so similar was because they were both copied from his own fake map!

Ajax was standing pale and silent behind Odilon, who could not contain his glee, while Ira stood to one side of Dolan, looking truculent. Quinn knew that Ajax had been horrified at having to use Quinn's stolen map, although it seemed that Ira wasn't much happier about it. Quinn knew that Ira probably thought his own work was superior, but that he'd been overruled by Dolan.

Now the three maps were displayed side by side on the

wall of the counting house – and Quinn's was markedly different from the other two.

Ignoring the whispering of the courtiers around him, Quinn's eyes traveled to the figure on Dolan's other side. Kurt looked smug, a small bag gripped in his right hand. Quinn had a good idea of what was in that bag and, given how closely Ira's map resembled Ajax's, just how Kurt had convinced Dolan to take him on board the *Wandering Spirit*.

Quinn's eyes moved to his beautiful, perfect, real map, alive with the colored inks that Ash had created for him. He was proud of his work. Ajax had added his own touches to Quinn's fake map, with exquisite illustrations, but Quinn still thought his looked better. But it was all for naught. Zain was going to lose the race because of Quinn's own fake map.

"My mapmaker kept two maps, sire," Zain was saying. "One of those disappeared during our journey – and these two look very similar to that map."

Quinn knew Zain couldn't outright accuse the other two explorers of taking Quinn's map – not without proof. And without Cleric Greenfield, there was no proof that Quinn had even made a fake map. Not for the first time in the past few weeks, Quinn found himself wishing his elderly friend was with him.

"So you say," said Odilon, mincing forward with an

obsequious smile. "But why should we take your word for it?"

"Why, indeed?" said Dolan, striding over to stand beside Odilon. "Take the word of a slave who would do anything to escape the chains that bind him?"

Zain raised one eyebrow in the King's direction at those words, but Quinn knew that he would say nothing, and neither would the King. Their roles had been set long ago and, without a win in the race, there was no reason to change them.

"Well, then," said the King, looking very unhappy. "I suppose we must then announce a winner." He sat back against the gilt-edged cushions that lined his throne, fingers steepled before him, deep in thought.

Queen Lorelei, in her matching gold throne beside him, leaned over and whispered to him.

"Oh, yes," he said, sitting upright once more. "The treasure. Did you find anything?"

Odilon stepped forward. "We have gold and this exquisite tapestry map, found in a distant, crumbling castle."

The King looked interested. Quinn rolled his eyes as the rug was brought forward. That tapestry map belonged to him as much as to Ajax, who'd been with him when they found it.

Dolan waited until Odilon had spread his treasures on the floor before the King. "Sire, we too have gold, and, sire, we have *these* . . ." He stepped back and, with a dramatic flourish, allowed a dozen or more starstones to cascade onto Odilon's tapestry in a glittering waterfall. There was a collective gasp of wonder from the crowd, and Quinn's fists clenched.

Kurt smirked at him, and it took Zain's calming hand on his arm to prevent Quinn from charging across the room to knock the smile from Kurt's face.

"Patience," Zain whispered.

"And you, Zain?" the King said hopefully.

"Sire, we too have starstones," Zain said, holding out the handful that Kurt had left behind. The crowd muttered, and Quinn could see that they were not as impressed as they had been by Dolan's display. "The remains of a larger collection that . . . disappeared from the *Libertas*."

The crowd muttered again, and Dolan studied the ceiling. The King frowned, but Zain said no more because, Quinn knew, how would he prove any allegations?

"And . . ." Zain continued, handing the King a small sack, "we take great pleasure in returning these to you."

The King reached inside and withdrew one of the large, perfect loganstones, holding it above his head so that it caught the light, scattering burnished yellow rays around the room. He gasped in surprise. "My mother's loganstones," he said. "I had never thought to see them again and yet here they are. How did you get them?"

"That is a story for another time," said Zain, and Quinn knew that he was protecting Tomas, who was waiting on the *Libertas* with the rest of the crew for the outcome of today's decision.

"He probably stole them in the first place," came a snooty, anonymous voice from somewhere behind Quinn, and Zain stiffened as Odilon and Dolan smiled. The people around Quinn laughed softly.

"I know that you had never seen them, as they were stolen before you arrived here," the King said pointedly to Zain, and the laughter near Quinn died abruptly. "But they were my dearest possessions and I thank you for their return."

Zain stepped back, but Ash nudged him. "We've got these too," she whispered fiercely.

"Do you have something to say, young man?" asked the King.

Ash, still in her breeches and looking like a cabin boy, stepped forward. "Only that we also have these," she said, walking towards the throne with an awkward head bob that Quinn thought was supposed to be a bow. Her arms were full and she announced each "treasure" to the room as she laid them at the foot of the throne.

"These are fruits," she said, putting down the little bowls. As soon as the weather had turned warmer, she'd replanted the seeds from the plants she'd picked up in the tribal village, and they were now lush green plants laden with tangy red fruit. "But they taste more savory than sweet."

"This," she said, walking over to the Queen and, with an awkward curtsey, handing her a small wooden box, "is *cacao* and it's the most delicious thing I've ever had in my mouth." The Queen smiled faintly and took it from her.

"And these," said Ash, putting three little packets next to her plants, "are ground powders, from roots and bark and dried leaves, I think, but with so much flavor that they'll transform anything in your palace kitchens." She and Cook had experimented with the powders in the *Libertas* galley, and Quinn had to admit she was right.

"Have you quite finished?" came a lazy drawl to Quinn's left, and Dolan stepped forward. "This is not treasure. Plants? Drinks? Powdered bark?"

Ash stood up straighter. "That all depends on your definition of treasure, Mr. Dolan," she said, and, with great dignity, bowed to the King and returned to Zain's side.

King Orel smiled down at her, eyes twinkling. "Thank you –" He stopped. "What is your name, boy?"

"This is Ash," said Zain, responding for her.

"And how exactly did Ash come to be in your company?" asked the King.

"Taken on as crew," said Zain, smoothly.

"Interesting," said the King. "I thought I'd perhaps seen you before. Must have been mistaken."

Zain nodded as Ash shrank behind him, hoping that the King wouldn't recognize her as the kitchen maid who'd disappeared without permission from his service one year before.

"Anyway, the loganstones do count for a great deal, but . . ." The King's eyes turned towards the glittering pile of starstones and Quinn knew that all was lost.

There was silence in the counting house, as though the crowd was holding its breath, knowing that the moment was upon them. The winner of the Great Race was about to be declared.

"In weighing up the maps, the deadline, the treasure . . ." The King's voice trailed away. "I have no choice but to award first prize in the Race to Map the World to . . . Odilon of Blenheim."

The King continued talking, but Quinn could hear nothing over the shrieks of the crowd and the roar of blood in his ears. The man who had arranged for Quinn's own kidnapping by Gelynions and stolen his map had been declared the winner.

He looked over at Ajax, who was standing beside his captain, looking miserable. Ira and Dolan were talking angrily to each other, gesturing towards the starstones.

The King thumped his scepter on the floor, and the crowd came to order. "Odilon of Blenheim crossed the finish line first, and his mapmaker Ajax is to be congratulated on a splendid map – Queen Lorelei particularly liked the fine drawings of the strange sea creatures."

Ajax blushed and shifted on his feet.

"But our treasure!" protested Dolan.

"Yes, your starstones are impressive," said the King. "I had heard of them, but never seen them and to see so many . . . but the fact remains that you were second, and that your map does not contain the fine line-work drawings of the other. On balance, Odilon has done more."

Unable to contain himself, Quinn moved to step forward – only to stop as Zain's big arm dropped across the front of his body, holding him back.

"But we can't just say nothing!" Quinn hissed.

"We have said our piece," said Zain, "and we have no more proof now than we had a few moments ago. You must let it go, Quinn. The truth has a way of outing itself in time."

"That will be too late!" said Quinn, bitterly. "Odilon will be on the Council and you will be stuck as the King's slave forever."

Zain nodded, and Quinn could finally see past his own burning disappointment to the sadness in his captain's eyes. "If we protest now, we will get nowhere," he said. "Patience."

Quinn shook his head in frustration, remembering having almost this exact conversation with Zain months earlier. "You cannot change what people will do," he'd said. "You can only change how you react to those things."

Zain had also talked about accepting things you couldn't change, rather than bashing your head against them over and over until you were senseless, but Quinn thought, looking over to where a jubilant Odilon was accepting the congratulations from what looked like the entire female population of the castle, he wouldn't mind bashing something right now.

"Go and speak to your friend," said Zain, breaking into Quinn's fury. "This is not his fault and he is feeling bad."

Quinn nodded. Taking a deep, calming breath, he strode across the room to Ajax, who was standing apart from his captain, looking dejected.

"Quinn, I'm –" Ajax floundered for the right words.

"I know," said Quinn, realizing that he couldn't take his anger out on his friend. "It's okay."

"It's not!" Ajax shouted, drawing questioning eyes towards them. He lowered his voice. "I feel terrible about using your map, and I have no idea what I'm going to do with the land that I've won. But Odilon told me that if I said anything he'd make sure I never went back to Cleric Fennelly – he'd see that I went back to the foster home and I'd have to stay there until I was sixteen." Ajax shook his head, sadly. "I couldn't do that, Quinn," he said. "I'm so sorry. The cleric will have missed me and . . . that place is like jail."

Quinn put his arm around his friend's shoulders. "It's not your fault, Ajax," he said. "Nobody is blaming you. And your drawings really *are* beautiful." He walked over to look at Ajax's map more closely.

"I love this one of Nammu," he said, tracing the outline with his finger. They had not seen "the great white beast" since she'd swum off with her baby, and he hoped they were both safe and happy.

"I'm glad you like it," said Ajax, "because I have this for you." He reached into his pocket, pulling out a leather thong.

"My tooth!" said Quinn, taking the animal tooth necklace from him. "I thought it was gone forever. Where did you find it?"

"I put it in my pocket without thinking after we opened Zain's cell door," said Ajax. "And then forgot all about it. But . . . have a closer look at it."

Quinn held the tooth up to the light and that's when he saw it. Etched onto the face of the long, pointed tooth was the delicate outline of Nammu, big tail pointing skyward, horn on her head.

"I used a sail-repair needle to scratch it into the surface," Ajax was saying, face anxious. "Do you like it?"

"I do," said Quinn, quietly, as he slipped the necklace over his head. "More than I can tell you."

Ajax grinned. "Well, that's a first then," he said. "Quinn Freeman lost for words."

Quinn smiled back. It had been a terrible day on so many levels, but at least he and Ajax were all right. And now he could take Nammu with him wherever he went. Even if the only place he was going was back to Markham.

Quinn sighed. "I guess it's time for me to go home," he said. "Mam and Da might have heard that we're back by now." Markham was a good day's travel by cart from Oakston, but words had a way of flying much faster.

"You don't sound very happy about it," said Ajax. "Particularly for someone who never wanted to leave home in the first place."

"I am happy," said Quinn, slowly. "I can't wait to see them all, but –"

"I know," said Ajax. "You wanted a different ending." He exhaled in frustration. "And you should have had one, Quinn. Your map is far and away the best but . . . why is it so different?"

"Oh," said Quinn absently, his mind on his family. "I made two. This is the real one. The one you used is fake."

Ajax whistled. "I knew it was a bit different from mine, but I just assumed I'd gotten it wrong because, well, because you were you."

"I'm sorry," said Quinn. "Anyone who uses your map or Ira's will end up running aground or getting hopelessly lost."

"You have to tell the King!" said Ajax, looking troubled. "They'll be sending out explorers based on this map."

"We tried to tell him!" said Quinn bitterly. "He won't listen. We have no proof, remember? He said my map is too different to be right." His rage was rising once again, and he could feel his face going red.

"What a mess," said Ajax, sadly. "Why didn't you tell anyone about it? Why isn't there anyone to stand up for you and say 'this is what really happened'?"

"I did tell someone," said Quinn, tears filling his eyes. "I told the cleric. But he died and the truth died with him."

Ajax was silent for a moment. "He'll be watching over you," he said softly.

Quinn's laugh was harsh. "Well, his last words to Ash were 'look up,' but it seems as though the cleric's off-duty at the moment," he said. "Otherwise we wouldn't be standing here like this."

"Look up?" said Ajax, eyebrows raised.

Quinn nodded.

"Strange. I –"

But whatever he was about to say was lost as a quavering voice interrupted them. "Ajax! My boy!"

Quinn turned to find a beaming cleric standing behind him. For a moment, it was as though Cleric Greenfield had returned, but, of course, it was not him.

"Cleric Fennelly!" cried Ajax, throwing himself at the elderly man.

"Ah, my boy, it's good to have you back!" said the

cleric, thumping Ajax on the back. "And I heard you are a winner! Let us go. You can tell me all about it at home!"

After that, there was no more to be said. The two boys hugged a fierce good-bye, and Ajax waved as he left the counting house, the cleric leaning heavily on his arm.

Quinn watched them go until Ajax's red hair was no longer visible.

"Quinn Freeman."

Quinn turned to face Zain.

"It is time to go," said Zain somberly. "There is a cart at the docks to take you and Tomas to Markham. Let us not make your mam wait a moment longer than she must."

Quinn nodded, throat aching as he tried to find the words to say good-bye. "I –" He broke off.

"You did well," Zain said. "But I expected no less. I think the only person you surprised was yourself."

Quinn managed a lopsided smile. "You told me I had something you needed," he said, "on that first day."

Zain smiled his familiar baring of teeth. "You did," Zain said. "I know that you think that I took you on board only for that extraordinary memory of yours, but that was not what I was talking about."

Quinn frowned. "Then what was it?"

Zain's hard face softened. "You were so committed to doing your duty, Quinn Freeman. You were so uncomfortable, so unhappy, but it did not stop you doing what you needed to do for your family."

"I was afraid," Quinn admitted softly, eyes on his boots, which looked even more tattered against the palace's gleaming black-and-white tiled floors.

"I know," Zain said. "But any man who thinks for himself will never be fearless. Yet the man who is afraid and faces the unknown because he must . . . That is a brave man. You showed a loyalty that I knew could not be beaten."

"And yet we were beaten." Again, the bitterness threatened to overwhelm Quinn.

"We were not beaten," said Zain, "we were robbed. There's a difference."

"*Leif's boots!*" Quinn erupted. "How can you be so calm?!"

"Oh, I am not calm," said Zain, and this time his smile was truly terrifying. "I am resigned. For now."

Quinn shook his head. The race was lost. It was over and he was going home to Markham. Better he leave now than spill the hot tears that he'd been suppressing since they'd first set foot in the counting room and he'd seen those other maps – *his* maps – tacked to the wall. "I think you're right, Zain," was all he said. "I think it's time for me to go home."

Zain looked at him. "About that . . ." he started.

Quinn waited.

"Once you've seen the world, you can never unsee it," said Zain. "You may find that home is not as you remembered."

Quinn laughed. "Of course it will be," he said. "I remember everything, *remember*?"

Zain smiled, though Quinn could see sadness in his eyes. "Perhaps," he said. "But we will meet again, Quinn Freeman. Of that I am sure."

Chapter Twenty

The cart ride to Markham passed in a blur. As the outskirts of Oakston faded into a sea of green fields, Quinn had retreated into his own thoughts as Tomas gazed about, openmouthed. As absorbed as he was, it took Quinn a long while to remember that, to Tomas, Verdania was as exotic as Barbarin had been to Quinn.

"Nearly there," he said, turning to Tomas, finally beginning to feel excitement breaking through his bad mood.

"It's so . . . organized," Tomas replied.

Quinn laughed, thinking of the riotous and voracious plant life that grew around Tomas's village in Barbarin. There, the landscape was only barely contained, and there was always the feeling that the lush green plants with their brightly colored fruits and flowers would take over if you looked away for a second.

Here, he thought, eyes scanning the neatly walled fields, the carefully plowed earth and the tidy cottages and barns dotting the landscapes, the people were in control.

As they drew into the village of Markham, doors of the whitewashed cottages began opening, and people stepped out to stare as they passed. Quinn realized they must look a fright. He was still wearing his patched breeches, his hair flopping over his eyes. Tomas was in one of the shirts his mother had packed for him – today's was a deep, rich red that stood out like a jewel against the gray sky.

"I do not like the heaviness of the sky," Tomas said, looking up. "It is always threatening rain but not delivering."

"Oh, it delivers," said Quinn with a laugh. "Days and days' worth of soft, pattering rain. Just you wait."

Tomas pulled his cloak closer. "Father did not mention that," he said. "Only the green fields."

"Home looks different from far away," said Quinn, realizing how true the words were even as he spoke them. When he'd missed Markham, he'd thought only of the good things. Now that he saw the villagers lined up, with their questioning eyes and, in some cases, a disapproving droop to their mouths, he remembered Sarina and Ash and how badly they'd been treated here.

Every place had its dangers, it's just that some were more subtle than others.

The cart rumbled to a stop in front of the Freeman's cottage just as the skies opened, and the rain began tumbling down. At first Quinn sat motionless, drinking in the sight of home. It looked smaller than he remembered.

Tomas nudged him. "Are we going in?" he asked, hood pulled closely over his head.

Even as he spoke, the front door burst open and Quinn's mam ran out. Heedless of the rain, arms open, her fierce joy radiated from her. "Quinn!" she shrieked. "Oh, Quinn."

He scrambled down from the cart and moments later was engulfed in warmth as she gathered him into a hug.

"Quinn," she murmured over and over, and it was nearly the undoing of him. Pictures flashed through his mind: the terror of his kidnapping, the darkness of the hold on the *Black Hawk*, the fury at having his map stolen (twice), the disappointment at not winning for his family, for Zain. It was almost worse reliving them while he was safe here with her. Almost.

"Oh, Mam," he said, hugging her back hard, his voice quavering. "We didn't win."

She stepped back, putting one hand on his face. "It doesn't matter," she said. "It's –"

Whatever she was about to say was lost in a great roar from behind him, as all five of his brothers joined them, having run from the barn, alerted by their mam's shrieks. They leapt on him, wrestling and rumbling, rubbing his hair, exclaiming in delight at his return. His da followed behind them, smiling.

"That's enough," he said, after a while, and Quinn was secretly relieved. He was thinking he'd received fewer bruises in his encounter with Morpeth than he had in this warm welcome from his brothers.

He walked over to his da.

"So, you're back," Beyard Freeman said.

"Yes, Da," said Quinn.

There was a moment's pause. Quinn wanted to give his da a big hug, but Beyard was not a demonstrative man as a rule. Besides . . .

"We didn't win, Da," said Quinn, eyes lowered. "I'm sorry."

Another pause, before his da reached out and dragged Quinn in for a short, fierce hug. "You did your best, Quinn," he said. "I know you did. And the money we received each month made a huge difference around here."

"I'm engaged now," said Simon, from behind him. "Thanks to you, Merry's da gave permission."

"We weathered some hard seasons well," his da continued. "We couldn't have done it without you."

Quinn managed a smile.

"Ahem," came a small voice from high on the cart seat.

"Oh, Mam, Da –" said Quinn. "This is Tomas. I said he could come and stay with us for a while."

His parents looked up at Tomas, with his caramel skin, dark, curly hair and bright-red shirt.

Quinn's da raised his eyebrows. "Where did you find him?"

Tomas got down from the cart. "I am from a kingdom known as Barbarin," he said in perfect Verdanian.

"Barbarin?" said Quinn's oldest brother, Jed. "Where's that?"

Quinn laughed. "The other side of the world! But it's a very long story . . ."

"Come inside, Tomas," said his mam. "Everyone, inside, out of the rain. Quinn has a lot to tell us."

Quinn looked at all of them, their beloved, familiar, expectant faces, and wondered how he could possibly make them understand the places he'd been, the things he'd seen.

How could he describe the harsh light of Deslond, dazzling and clear? Or how the ocean was not one shade of blue, but a changeling creature of grays and greens and even fiery reds when the sun lay on the horizon?

Could they ever comprehend that people could live in caves lit by starstones? Or that the very air changed scent as it flowed over different coastlines? Even now his nose wrinkled as he thought of the smell of the fecund earth of Barbarin.

He thought of the desolate castle they'd visited, where desperate people had tried carving a new life out of the frozen ground, and the tribal village, with its gardens and livestock – not that different from Markham if you discounted the tentlike structures . . .

His mind threw up images of the huge wrinkled creature with the bedsheet ears, the *pescarn* with their snapping jaws, the vast schools of silvery fish that had seemed to race the *Libertas*, flashing in and out of the water like arrows, the flocks of birds that flew so thickly overhead some days that they blocked out the very sun.

In that moment, Quinn missed Ash, Ajax, Zain and the others who'd shared the journey, who *knew*, with the same sharpness he'd felt on board the *Libertas* when he'd thought about his family.

Would he feel divided like this forever now? he wondered as, surrounded by his brothers who were all talking at once, he followed his parents inside.

⁓

Quinn yawned, long and loud, pushing his hands into the soft dough, kneading and pulling, pushing and stretching. Just two days in, and it was already as though he'd never left home, back in his role of youngest brother, in the kitchen.

Looking up from his task, he gazed out through the open door at the green fields beyond. He could see Jed and Allyn, ankle deep in dark-brown loam in the nearest field, deep in conversation, Tomas watching on with great interest. The trio had gone out that morning with buckets of seed, planting for the autumn harvest, but it looked as though they were doing more talking than planting. Allyn's new knife glinted on his belt, and Quinn's hand crept up to his tooth necklace at the sight, leaving a trail of flour across his shirt.

Allyn had been so taken with the tooth that he'd even offered to trade his knife for it, but Quinn had refused. He still had no knife of his own, but he would rather wait another year than give up Nammu. It was Allyn, however, who had suggested rubbing soot into Ajax's little carving, to make it stand out more, and Quinn was grateful for that.

A gentle breeze rustled the honeysuckle planted around the door, and a waft of the sweet, heady scent tickled his nose. On the other side of the warm, sunny kitchen, his mam hummed as she stoked the fire, making it flare up before dying back to the hot, glowing coals she needed to bake the bread he was kneading.

It was all just as Quinn had dreamed so many times when he was lonely and homesick on the *Libertas*.

"Oh, Quinn, I nearly forgot," his mam said, buzzing around him. She was still constantly finding excuses to touch him, reaching out to ruffle his hair or tweak his collar or – anything that allowed her to reassure herself that he was really here. "I made you something while you were away. Just to – well, you know."

Stave off thoughts that you weren't coming back at all, he finished for her silently.

She reached into the big basket she kept tucked beside the fire, bringing out a pile of moss-colored felted wool. "It's a tunic," she said, handing it to him. "For winter. I made it a little bigger, to allow for growth, but . . . try it on."

Putting the dough aside to rise, he dusted off his hands before pulling the soft wool on over his shirt, feeling the love she'd put into every stitch. Popping his head through the neck, he pushed his arms down the sleeves . . .

"I think it will go beautifully with your eyes . . . oh," his mam said. "You've grown so much!"

Quinn looked down at his wrists, hanging out of the bottom of the tunic sleeves. The wool stretched across his chest, and rode up at the hemline.

"So I have," he said, in wonder. Despite his mam's best efforts, he was still wearing his clothes from the *Libertas*, even the patched breeches. He and Tomas had let her trim their hair after his da had made pointed jokes about having "savages" under his roof, but Quinn just wasn't yet ready to let go of his clothes, even though they were so tattered after a year at sea that he hadn't even noticed he'd outgrown them!

"Oh well, I'll let it out," she said, with a laugh. "And down."

Later, tucked up in his old bed beneath the eaves, his brother Allyn snoring a few footsteps away, Quinn reflected that it wasn't just that tunic that didn't fit right anymore. He was enjoying his time with his mam, his role as the youngest, protected brother – but he also knew that his family couldn't see the real Quinn anymore. The Quinn who'd survived storms and pirates and tribal attacks; the Quinn who'd longed for his brothers to have his back – but who'd still managed to fight for himself.

They would always see him as Little Quinn, but Quinn knew that while he only seemed a little bigger on the outside, inside he was oceans away from the boy who'd left home.

"Once you've seen the world, it can never be unseen," Zain had said.

It seemed that his captain was right. *Again*.

~

"Quinn!"

Quinn looked up from his notebook, cocking his head to better hear who was shouting his name. He had tucked himself up in the hayloft, in a comfortable bed of straw, looking for some peace and quiet. He'd been home seven days now, and it confounded him how it could be harder to find time alone here than it had been when he was confined to a ship, but it was. Someone was always looking for him. It was as though, having missed him for a year, they needed to have him in sight at all times.

211

"Quinn!" It was Jed, and his voice was now rising with impatience. Quinn sighed. His oldest brother would not give up and walk away like Heath or Berrick would. No, Jed would keep looking until Quinn's hiding place was unearthed and then give Quinn an earful for ignoring him.

"Coming!" he shouted in resignation, tucking the notebook into the back of his breeches, and picking up the other books he'd stacked next to him in anticipation of several hours' reading. Cleric Redlands had welcomed him back with open arms, thrilled that his source of Mistress Freeman's jams and preserves had returned. In fact, he'd turned up on the doorstep with an armload of books and a hopeful expression the day after Quinn got home.

Quinn slithered one-armed down the ladder from the hayloft, smiling as he thought of his brothers' surprise at his new skills. Just yesterday, Simon had watched, open-mouthed, as Quinn had shinnied up the drainpipe to rescue one of his mam's dusting cloths, which had blown up there in a gust of wind. And all five of them were now enthusiastic participants in the training sessions that he and Tomas hadn't even thought *not* to continue now that they were not on the *Libertas*.

At first the Freeman brothers had laughed, as he and Tomas had gone through their warm-up routine, but they'd quickly become interested once the sparring began, begging Quinn to teach them the Deslondic fighting system. Quinn had now experienced the supreme pleasure of putting Allyn flat on his back on several occasions. He had noticed, though, that his brother was a quick learner – it wouldn't be long before he had some countermoves of his own.

"I'm here," Quinn said now, emerging from the barn to find an exasperated Jed standing, hand on hips, scanning the yard.

"You've got a visitor," said Jed, turning on his heel and striding back to the house. "You're to come at once."

A visitor? Quinn followed, thoughtfully. Last time visitors had arrived unexpectedly, Quinn had found himself swallowed up in a grand adventure. His pace quickened, and, thrusting the good cleric's books into his brother's arms, he ran past Jed, into the house – and straight into Ajax.

"What are you doing here?!" Quinn exclaimed in delight.

"I've been sent to fetch you," said Ajax, with a huge smile at this friend. "All of you. We're to go right now."

And that was all he would say, despite Quinn's best efforts to draw him out, all the way to Oakston.

Not that there'd been much talking on the journey. Quinn's eyes had widened at the carriage sent to fetch them all – one of the King's own, no less – and its grandeur had the effect of subduing even Allyn. But Quinn's mind raced with questions, and he could see his parents communicating their own anxiety to each other in that wordless way they had.

What was going on?

Chapter Twenty-one

This time the counting room was much less crowded, giving Quinn the space to take in the grandeur of its gilt panels, the golden thrones, the trumpeter standing in his gilt-edged uniform by the door, just as he remembered from Decision Day. Three liveried servants stood, silent and still, next to the King's throne.

The Freemans huddled close together to the left of the great hall, creating a solid cluster. Standing between Jed and Simon, Quinn looked across the hall to Ira, who was accompanied by an impressive-looking gray-haired man dressed in a velvet tunic. Quinn would have taken him for a courtier, in the style of Odilon, but his worn leather boots and the sword at his hip suggested a fighting man at heart. He bore a strong resemblance to Ira, and Quinn surmised that this was Lord Thornten himself.

Ira stood a little apart from his father, staring coldly around the room. Quinn stared back at him and was gratified to note that Ira's eyes dropped when they met his, though whether this was because Ira was remembering their last encounter or because Ira had seen the size and sheer number of Quinn's brothers, he wasn't sure.

The trumpeter sounded three sharp notes, and Odilon of Blenheim strutted into the room, wearing soft satin slippers and those ludicrously puffy pants that Quinn remembered from their first encounter. He was accompanied by two giggling ladies. Quinn was surprised by the look of unease on Odilon's haughty face – perhaps being a member of the King's Council wasn't as much fun as he'd thought it would be?

When Dolan arrived next, with Kurt at his heels, however, Quinn began to realize that they were all there about the race. The question was, why? Dolan took his place in the center of the room and they all stood in quiet unease. Quinn's da coughed, and the sound echoed around the room even as his mam dug her elbow into his side.

Then the trumpeter sounded a long, loud fanfare and the King entered, with that same strange wince at the sound that Quinn had noticed the first time he'd seen the King. And then Zain came through the door, and Quinn smiled.

"We will meet again, Quinn Freeman," Zain had said, and so it was.

Zain looked across at him and slowly and deliberately

winked, though his face remained impassive. Did Zain know why they were all here?

The King's next words dispelled that thought. "Thank you all for coming here today," he said, as though any of them had a choice to ignore his command. "I know that you're all wondering why you're here – well, all except Ajax – but be patient."

So Ajax *did* know more than he'd let on. Quinn noticed that his friend had been quietly joined by Cleric Fennelly, who was beaming at the room, and that Master Blau had also joined them. Quinn was suddenly glad that he'd traveled all the way to Oakston with his notebook tucked into the back of his breeches – though it hadn't been comfortable. He knew the master would enjoy reading the notes that Quinn had taken throughout the journey – even those very first "no land today" entries.

Quinn also knew that the good master would make excellent use of all the information contained within its pages, from the maps of the stars that Quinn had drawn, to the descriptions of the wild and wonderful animals and plants that he and Ash had deliberated over. At least some use would come of all their efforts.

"Baldwin, fetch the maps," the King commanded, bringing Quinn's thoughts back to the matter at hand. One of the servants quickly left the room, reappearing moments later to tack the three world maps up on the wall where the King – and everyone else – could see them.

Quinn felt a pang at the sight of his beautiful map, the product of so many hours of hard work, feeling that horrible disappointment welling up inside him once again.

"Which one is yours?" Jed whispered.

"The one in the middle," responded Quinn, forlornly.

Jed studied it. "It looks good, but it's different from the others," he said. "How did you make those colors?"

"Ash made them." He'd told his family all about Ash's role in the journey, and the boys had been full of admiration for her exploits, though Quinn had noticed his mother frowning a little.

The King was speaking again. "Eight days ago, Odilon of Blenheim was named as winner of the Race to Map the World," he said. "However . . ."

He paused, and Quinn heard a ripple of whispers throughout the room.

"Certain information has come to light that suggests that Odilon of Blenheim's map, although beautifully illustrated –" the King broke off to nod to Ajax, who smiled back. "Although beautifully illustrated is not *accurate* – and therefore must be discounted from consideration."

"What?" Odilon erupted. "How can you say that? Dolan's map is almost exactly the same." Dolan, who had perked up considerably at the King's words, looked daggers at him.

"Indeed," said the King, frowning at the interruption. "But Dolan's map is also inaccurate."

Lord Thornten looked down at Ira, who was now staring at his own shuffling feet.

Quinn's eyes flew to Zain, who remained impassive. Taking his cue from his captain, Quinn also stood, face as blank as he could manage.

"Bah!" said Odilon. "What is this information? Whatever it is, it is not true and cannot be trusted."

"Oh," said the King, nodding to Cleric Fennelly, who stepped forward. "I think it can. The letters please, cleric."

And Cleric Fennelly pulled, from some deep inner pocket in his plain brown robes, a small pile of folded vellum tied with twine.

Quinn's mouth dropped open – he knew what that pile was. Cleric Greenfield's letters, the ones that everyone on board the *Libertas* had always thought so humorous (after all, where would he mail them?) had come to light.

"These letters," the King said, taking them from the cleric, "were found in the cabin of Cleric Greenfield, who is no doubt looking down on us all right now asking, 'What took you so long?'"

It was as though the entire room held its breath as he untied the twine slowly.

"And they tell a very interesting story . . ."

Quinn could see both Dolan and Odilon swallow hard. "A tale of stolen food and treachery," said the King, looking hard at Dolan and Ira. "A tale of stolen maps and assisted kidnapping," he continued, and Odilon blushed to the roots of his hair. "But perhaps of most interest given the purpose of the journey," said the King, pulling out one piece of vellum, "a tale of two maps – one real and accurate and hidden, one fake and inaccurate and . . . twice stolen."

"They're the fakes!" shrieked Odilon, pointing at the letters. "How can they be real? Why weren't they brought to your attention at the end of the race?"

Ajax stepped forward, eyeing his captain with active dislike. "They couldn't be found," he said. "It wasn't until I was discussing Cleric Greenfield's last words with Cleric Fennelly that we realized. 'Why would he say look up?' I asked. 'Is there some spiritual significance to that?' And the cleric laughed at me. 'No,' he said. 'Cleric Greenfield was never one to mince his words. He wanted you to look up.'

"So we went to Cleric Greenfield's cabin on the *Libertas*, and we looked up," said Cleric Fennelly, with the relish of an old man who had the attention of the room. "And there they were, hidden behind a loose board above the cleric's bed. Quite why he saw the need to hide them, I'm not sure, but I'm thinking he just liked to have them close by – or maybe he had reasons not to trust anyone."

The room erupted, with everyone talking at once. Quinn's heart beat faster – what did this all mean?

"So," said the King, "it seems that some changes must be made."

Quinn looked once more to Zain, who had not yet moved. This time Zain caught his eye, and again came that slow wink. Quinn felt as though the smile he gave in response might split his face in two.

"Odilon, step forward," said the King, in a tone that brooked no argument. Odilon minced forward, and Quinn noted that the two ladies were no longer giggling and had moved away towards the door.

"You have no place on my Council," the King continued, waving the letters in his right hand. "You are hereby stripped of your seat and I suggest that you return to that tiny estate of yours in the west country and stay there for a good long while. If I see you again, you will lose your lands as well."

Odilon managed a shaky bow before retreating from the hall, walking backward, his eyes never leaving the King.

Ajax looked as though he wanted to cheer.

"Dolan," snapped the King. Dolan stepped forward, eyes on the black-and-white tiled floor. "It seems to me that you need some time to think. Men who steal from fellow Verdanians are not men I want near me. So . . ."

The King paused, tapping his fingers on the stack of letters.

"You will go to the docks and board the *Wandering Spirit*," he said, finally. "The oceans beyond the northern countries need further exploration. And take *that boy* with you." He indicated Kurt, who did not understand what was being said, but cowered nonetheless at the expression on the King's face. "He merits special mention by Cleric Greenfield, and I think the two of you are well matched."

Dolan, face white under his tan as he contemplated months and months at sea in blustery, icy conditions, opened his mouth to speak – and quickly closed it at the King's expression. He turned, dragging Kurt by the arm.

Quinn could see the blond boy asking Dolan, in Suspite, what was happening, because, of course, he'd never bothered to try to pick up the Verdanian language during his time on board the *Libertas*. Quinn couldn't help but feel a surge of glee at the thought of the long, freezing, uncomfortable days Kurt had before him . . .

"And now we come to Zain."

Zain bowed.

"And to the mapmakers."

Quinn looked around, noticed that Ajax and Ira had both stepped forward, and hastily did the same.

The room was silent, all eyes on the King, who was once again tapping his steepled fingers, though this time his eyes were on the huge oak doors behind the trumpeter.

"Baldwin," he said, suddenly. "Open those doors – and you, Fred, no fanfare." The trumpeter nodded, lowering his instrument.

Baldwin strode across to the doors, flinging them open – and the sizeable crowd of castle residents who'd clearly been clustered around it, hoping to listen in, tried desperately to look as though they were just passing by.

"Come in," said the King, with a hint of exasperation. "On this occasion, I want no half-truths and rumors flying down the castle corridors. I want this heard."

Shamefaced, the courtiers, servants, councilors, lords and ladies filed into the hall.

"Move forward," the King said to the Freemans, who shuffled up behind Quinn and Zain, while the crowd pressed in behind them. "Hear this," said the King, then waited patiently while the trumpeter sounded the three-note proclamation song. "I do solemnly declare that Zain of Deslond is the true and only winner of the Race to Map the World, having conducted himself with honor, bravery and diligence – the only man to have done so."

There was a gasp from the crowd, and a great babble of voices rose.

"Enough!" roared the King, and even the trumpeter was silent. "I award Zain not only his freedom, which has been by rights his for many years –" A wave of whispers broke out at this statement, cut off abruptly by the King's hard stare. "But the new place on the Council recently vacated by Odilon of Blenheim."

This time there was no containing the cacophony of surprise and discussion. Zain remained unperturbed, nodding with dignity to the King, whose face was wreathed in smiles. "You have been," the King continued, raising his voice above the din, "a true friend and a trusted advisor over many years and I can think of no one else I would rather have at my right hand."

Quinn struggled to contain his joy, so happy was he for his captain, and he could see that even Zain was battling to maintain his composure.

"I thank you, my King," he said, slowly, and the two men shared a long, warm look of understanding.

"But," said King Orel, turning back to the room, "this leaves me with a dilemma. As you all know, the winning mapmaker receives a parcel of land in addition to his monetary prize, and it would pain me to remove that from Ajax, particularly when he has done so much to resolve the cheating and deception we have witnessed."

He paused, eyes searching the room. They came to rest on the Freemans, and his face softened as he caught sight of Quinn's mother, surrounded by her husband and sons. "Mistress Freeman," he said, "would you mind taking a step forward?"

Flustered, she smoothed her hair and her skirts before doing so. Quinn's heart ached as the eyes of the court turned to her and he knew they were judging her plain cotton gown, stitched by her own hand, just as Ira had once looked down upon Quinn for his homespun tunics.

But his mother, pink cheeked, held her head high, and in that moment he could see the noble heritage that she never, ever talked about.

"You are Ellyn, daughter of Ralf, who was Baron of Cowl?"

"I am, sire," she said, quietly.

"Tell me again what happened to your father," said the King, though Quinn, remembering the conversation that he'd had with the King on the very first day they'd met, knew that he was already aware of the story.

"My father had only one child," said Ellyn. "Despite the fact that I was his daughter, not a son, he brought me up to run the estate, teaching me every aspect. When he fell ill, he made a petition to the King, your father, for special dispensation to change the inheritance laws."

Quinn gasped. Everyone knew that women could not inherit property. It was how it had always been.

"And my father said 'no,'" said King Orel quietly.

"It broke my father's heart," said Ellyn, and Quinn detected an unusual hint of bitterness in his mother' voice. "He died three days later, and the entire estat small though it was, was inherited by a distant cous who ordered that I depart immediately. I –"

She broke off, visibly distressed, and Quinn step over to hold her hand.

"Go on," said the King.

"I had nowhere to go," she said finally, gath herself to stand even taller. "I had no family and r wanted to know me after my father had tried som so unusual. So I packed a bag and left. I was lucky to be taken in by a freehold farmer's wife, Beyard's mother, and I have lived a fortunate life with him and my family ever since."

"And the distant cousin?"

"I don't know," she said. "He was never named in my presence and, from what I could gather, already had extensive lands on the other side of the kingdom. I'm not sure he's ever visited my father's manor house."

The King sat back against his velvet throne cushions, a small smile playing on his lips. "I suspected as much," he said. "As it turns out, I know your distant cousin . . ."

Again, a ripple of whispers ran through the hall like a river.

"In fact," said the King, sitting forward once more and clearly enjoying himself. "He – or rather, his son – is standing in this room."

Quinn's mother gasped, and everyone in the crowd began eyeing the people standing on either side.

"Lord Thornten," said the King, and the nobleman froze, "this is your distant second cousin, Ellyn."

The room erupted into a storm of exclamations. Quinn could feel his mother shaking as she stared across the room at Ira's father. Quinn's mind was whirling. If Lord Thornten and his mother were related, then that meant . . .

Ira was clearly doing the same calculations, for he'd gone white as a sheet and was shaking his head in silent protest, looking as though he might faint.

Quinn couldn't help but smile. For Ira to be related to the farm boy he so looked down upon and despised . . . another wave of glee ran through him, and he turned to look at Zain, who was baring his teeth with mirth. Zain knew as well as Quinn did that this was the greatest form of punishment for someone like Ira.

"Ira Thornten," the King said, raising his voice once again over the noise, which subsided immediately. "It seems to me that you have been led astray by your captain to a certain point."

Ira nodded, looking relieved. Perhaps his indiscretions were going to be overlooked.

"But," the King continued, "I can make no excuses for your other behavior. Ajax told me about the pit in that savage, foreign land and your heartlessness in allowing a fellow mapmaker to fall into Gelynion hands."

Ira shrank under the fierce condemnation in his King's eyes.

"For that reason – and just because, I have to say, it pleases me to do so – I am ordering that you atone for your actions."

Lord Thornten's face was thunderous, knowing that any atonement his son was to make would be coming from the Lord's own coffers.

"And so, I declare that the estate known as Selvidge Manor will be transferred, in its entirety, into the name of . . . Quinn Freeman, and will serve as the 'parcel of land' promised to the winning mapmaker as his prize."

"No!" shouted Lord Thornten, striding towards the throne, red with rage. "You cannot do this!"

The King sat bolt upright on his throne, face hard, and stared down at the angry Lord. "Oh, can't I?" he said silkily. "I can, you know – and more. Is that what you want, Lord Thornten?"

Quinn, who'd only ever seen the King as an affable man, suddenly saw in him the steel that had allowed him to face down Zain on a charging horse and calmly ask him to tea.

Lord Thornten, clearly seeing the same thing, stopped midstride, clenching and unclenching his fists, as he appeared to reconsider. Finally, he backed away, head lowered, muttering, "As you wish, sire."

"Lovely," said the King, back to his smiling self and rubbing his hands together. "Then let it be done."

Even through his shock, Quinn became aware that his mother was squeezing his hand so hard that it was turning blue. And he knew that there was one more thing to do. Or try to do.

"Er, Sire, Your Highness?" he asked timidly.

"Quinn? You wish to speak?" asked the King in surprise.

"Er, yes," he said, giving his mam's hand one last squeeze before walking towards the throne. "I was wondering if it would be all right if I, well, if my mam and I shared the estate."

Quinn wanted her to have the satisfaction of knowing it had come back to her – not just through him, her son, but to her. The birthright that the grandfather he'd never known had tried so hard to give her. Watching Ash fight for her place in a world dominated by men and boys had given him the courage to at least try to do this for his mam.

The King paused, thinking. "You wish to appoint your mother steward of your estate?" he said. "It's unusual, but I can think of no valid reason why that could not be done, given you are not yet a man."

Quinn smiled as his mam began weeping softly. But then his brothers launched themselves as one body, throwing themselves on Quinn in delight, simultaneously trying to rub his hair, hug him, slap him on the back and generally wrestle him to the ground. Fighting his way to the top of the pack, dragging in air, Quinn could see his father gather his mother to him in a long, gentle hug as she wept and wept.

All around them, people were talking, shouting, gesticulating, gossiping, and pushing forward to congratulate him. Quinn struggled to make sense of any of it. All he knew was that all the effort he'd put into creating a beautiful, perfect map had paid off.

He scrambled to his feet, looking for Zain, who was standing nearby, watching Quinn's brothers in wonder, before Quinn caught his eye.

"Well, Quinn Freeman, it appears you are a landowner," said Zain, with a twinkle in his eyes.

"And you are a trusted King's councilor," Quinn responded.

They stood in silence for a moment, taking in the celebrations around them. Quinn noticed that Lord Thornten was striding from the room, dragging a chastened Ira by the ear. Looking at the nobleman's stormy face, Quinn felt a small twinge of pity for Ira. He wouldn't like to be going home to Ira's castle tonight.

"Don't feel bad for him," said Zain, following his gaze. "He deserves everything he gets – and he will be back. His kind always is."

"And now," the King commanded, "everyone will clear the hall and go back to whatever task they *should* be undertaking. Except . . ." He turned to the Freemans. "Perhaps you will join us for high tea?" he asked, politely, and Beyard Freeman nodded mutely.

"And you, Zain, of course," said the King. "And Ajax and Cleric Fennelly. That should –"

He broke off as Zain stepped forward. "I think that Quinn and I would like to add a few more guests to the party," he said. "If it pleases Your Highness."

The King laughed. "Do I really have a choice?"

Zain bared his teeth in a ferocious smile. "Of course, sire," he said. "You are the King after all."

The King rolled his eyes. "Very well," he said. "Who shall we add?"

~

Cleaver mopped his brow with his red bandanna, looking as though he'd rather be on the *Libertas* fighting Gelynions than trying to discuss the weather with Queen Lorelei. Quinn watched as Ash, in a long dress the color of the summer sky, made her way over to Cleaver, slid her arm into his, and began talking to the Queen about *cacao* – a subject on which Her Highness was most enthusiastic, judging by her excited chatter. Cleaver's expression suggested Ash had pulled off a great rescue.

There was no way the Gelynions would have mixed him and Ash up today, Quinn thought with a smile, before turning to approach the chair where Master Blau was sitting, watching the proceedings as though studying human behavior.

"Ah, young Quinn," he said as Quinn sat down beside him. "My most promising pupil."

"You say that now," said Quinn, with a laugh.

"I always knew it," the master replied with a smile. "I was just waiting for you to see it."

Quinn blushed. "I am returning your gift," he said, pulling the notebook from the small of his back.

"Oh," said the master, taking it in his hand and turning it over. The leather cover was weather-stained and worn. "You did not find it useful?"

"I did," said Quinn, "and now I thought that you might find it useful."

Master Blau pulled at the leather thong that bound the book together, opening it to reveal the vellum pages, covered in Quinn's handwriting, with drawings and diagrams throughout. A pressed flower fell from the pages.

"Oh," he said, "this is a gift indeed. But I cannot keep this, Quinn. This is a record of your journey."

"I would not have made the journey without you," said Quinn. "And you are the only person I can think of who will read every word of this and . . . understand."

Master Blau gave him a long look. "I do understand," he said. "In my younger days, I too went out to make maps. I know that returning with the world in your head to a place where nothing has changed can be one of the most difficult parts of any journey."

He tapped the cover of the notebook. "I will read this," he said. "I will take in every word and every thought. And then I will return it to you in Markham and we will eat your mother's excellent cake and talk about it. What say you?"

Quinn couldn't help but smile at the thought. "I say yes," he said.

"I suspect Quinn will be far happier to see you in his home next time than he was during our last visit," said a deep voice behind him.

"Well," said Quinn, turning to face Zain, "at least next time I'll be expecting him."

Master Blau laughed. "Indeed," he said. "But now I am going to take my prize and retire to my rooms. I have an adventure to enjoy."

He was already poring over the pages as he walked, bumping into people as he made his way from the room.

"So, Quinn Freeman, it seems we have won."

"You always use my last name," Quinn said, without thinking. "Why do you do that?"

Zain laughed. "Because you have one," he said. "So few people in my world do."

Quinn nodded, taken aback. He hadn't thought of the value of his surname, but he realized that he'd never heard one in association with anyone else on the *Libertas*.

"A surname is a label of family, of roots," Zain was saying. "I know how important both of those things are to you." Quinn's eyes turned to where his brothers were sitting shoulder to shoulder at a long table that seemed to groan under the weight of the iced cakes, flaky pastries and jewellike sweets that covered it. His mother and father stood hand in hand in a corner, talking quietly and looking lighter and brighter than he could ever remember.

Quinn didn't know what to say, and Zain seemed to sense it.

"Speaking of family," he said, half turning to create space beside him, "this is my wife, Sia."

Quinn shook hands with the elegant, golden-skinned woman, who held herself like a princess. "And this," Zain said, putting his arm around a slim, tall girl of around thirteen, "this is Lena."

Quinn nodded awkwardly.

"We've heard about lot about you," said Sia.

"I've –" Quinn stopped. The truth was that he'd heard next to nothing about Zain's family.

"Third rule of the sea," said Zain with a wink. "Never discuss your family with sailors."

"Oh?" said Quinn, concentrating hard and managing to raise one eyebrow. "Is that written in a book somewhere?"

Zain laughed. "In the same one you found that information that saved Aysha, I'd imagine," he said, face straight.

"Did I hear my name?" Ash appeared beside Lena, who smiled at her, with Tomas at her heels.

"You and the Queen seem to be getting along," said Quinn, glad of the distraction.

"She loved the *cacao* I gave her," said Ash, "and agrees with me that it is, indeed, something to treasure. When she found out that Tomas knew all about how it was grown

234

and made, he became a treasure as well. She wants him to come and work here in the gardens."

Tomas blushed, though Quinn could see he looked pleased at the invitation. "I told her she will have to wait until a ship goes back to Barbarin to get some more, and some seeds, and she went off immediately in search of the King to get that organized. So I'll be staying with you a little longer, if that's all right, Quinn?" he said.

Quinn couldn't help but smile with relief. The thought of returning to Markham without Tomas and having no one to share his memories with had filled him with horror.

"Are you still here, in the gardens, Ash?" Quinn asked, changing the subject. He hadn't even had a chance to speak to her.

"I'm here, but not in the gardens," she said. "Zain arranged for me to live with him, Sia and Lena. He even lets me wear my breeches when we are in our quarters."

"And I want a pair too!" said Lena.

"Hmmph," said Zain. "We shall see about that."

Sia just smiled, and Quinn got the impression that Zain didn't often say no to Lena – which was an interesting notion.

"Quinn, it's time for us to go." Quinn turned to find his mother and father standing behind him. "We have so much to talk about, to think through," said his father.

Quinn nodded. Looking around, he saw that the *Libertas* crew was making their way from the hall, waving cheerfully as they went. Queen Lorelei had disappeared, probably to organize her supply of *cacao* and the King was staring intently at Quinn's map.

Torn at the thought of leaving his friends, but looking forward to some quiet time to think about this wonderful, confusing, overwhelming day, Quinn hesitated.

"Thank you," his father continued, stepping forward to take Zain's hand. "Thank you for everything."

"No," said Zain. "Thank you. We would not have won without your son, so I owe you a great debt."

Quinn's mother put her arm around him. "Any debt was paid when you brought him home safe to us," she said, and Zain acknowledged her words with a small bow.

"Ahem, I was wondering if –" Ajax had joined the group, looking embarrassed. "That is –" He shuffled his feet, before taking a steadying breath. "Mr. Freeman, I am no farmer," he said. "Cleric Fennelly and I were wondering if we might draw on your expertise with the management of my land. I do not wish to leave him again so soon and . . . well, I wondered if you and your sons might be willing to assist us. For a fee, of course," he finished in a rush.

Beyard Freeman scratched his head. "I never thought I'd see the day I'd be managing three different farms," he said. "I always knew there was a reason we were blessed with so many boys. Of course, we'll help young Ajax – and no fee. None of us would be in this position were it not for you and your very clever cleric."

Ajax smiled his hundred-deckert grin, and the room felt warmer. "I thought it would mean that we'd all need to see each other quite regularly as well?" he said, hopefully.

Quinn's mother laughed. "I'm sensing an ulterior motive here," she said. Quinn thought she looked ten years younger than she had when they'd arrived at the castle that morning, and realized in that moment just how difficult the loss of her father, and the circumstances around that loss, had been for her. It was *almost* worth being the subject of Ira's heartlessness to see her like this.

"The King is sending us home in his carriage," said Quinn's father. "Walk with me, Ajax, and we'll talk about it." As they left, accompanied by Quinn's brothers, and with Cleric Fennelly, Ash, Lena and Sia following, all eager to say good-bye, Quinn found himself, for the second time in his life, alone with Zain and the King.

"Well, Zain," said the King, still staring at Quinn's map. "Were you happy with your choice of mapmaker?"

Quinn remembered the King asking Zain this question over a year ago at Decision Day.

"I knew he'd do," said Zain, and Quinn rolled his eyes, recognizing Zain's words. "And he did."

The King laughed. "Indeed, he did. I look forward to using your map as the basis of further exploration, Quinn."

Quinn smiled, as the idea that his map would be *used* really hit home.

"I know that you were not . . . an enthusiastic participant of the race," the King continued. "But perhaps one day you will join another expedition?"

Quinn bowed, buying time as he considered the King's question, thinking of all that had happened on this journey, all he had seen, all he had felt, all he had learned. "You know, Your Highness," he said slowly. "I think that perhaps one day I will."

But now, he was ready to go home.

At least for a while.

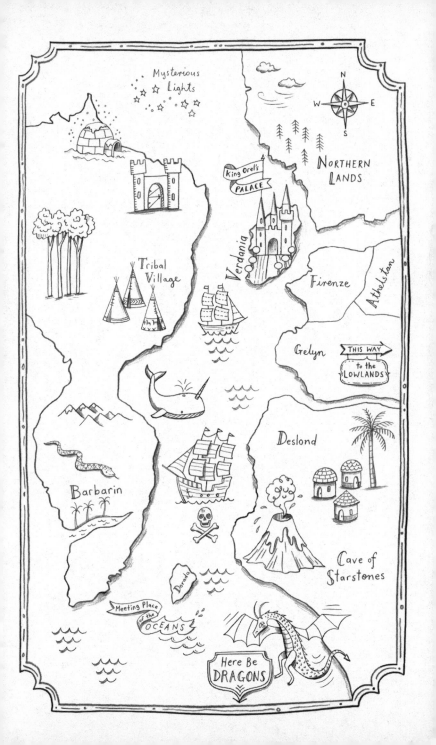

Collect the Whole Series

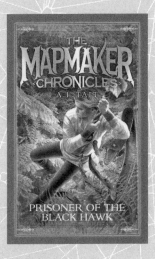

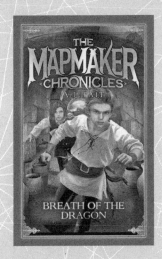

A. L. Tait, who writes fiction and nonfiction for adults under another name, grew up dreaming of world domination. Unfortunately, at the time there were only alphabet sisters B. L. and C. A. and long-suffering brother M. D. M. to practice on . . . and parents who didn't look kindly upon sword fights, plank walking or thumbscrews. But dreams don't die and The Mapmaker Chronicles, the author's first series of books for children, is the result.

A. L. Tait lives in country NSW, Australia, with a family, a garden, four goldfish and a very cheeky puppy.